"Hi a

"Hi," they said .... and shared a look. God, this hunk of man needed to get out of her line of vision soon. An urge to bite something taunted her. She plucked a fry from her dish and bit off the end with her front teeth.

"Enjoy the rest of your day," he said with that slanty mouth of his.

After he strode by, leaving a waft of pine-forest scent in his wake, Rylee pulled her gaze over to Kit, who stared back with round eyes. "What?"

"You should see what you look like right now, pal."

Rylee reached up to touch her own cheek, which was hot from the flame of him.

"I've never seen you react to a guy like that."

Now that he was gone, she swallowed hard and breathed in the leftover spiciness in the air. Yeah, that guy had to stay gone.

Praise for M. Kate Quinn

SUMMER IRIS was a Finalist for The Golden Quill Award;

MOONLIGHT & VIOLET won The Golden Leaf Award; and

BROOKSIDE DAISY was a (TWRP) Finalist for The Golden Leaf Award

~*~

"M. Kate Quinn fully captures the reader's heart."

~Long and Short Reviews

Saying Yes
to the Mess

by

M. Kate Quinn

Sycamore River Series

Saying Yes to the Mess

COPYRIGHT © 2018 by M. Kate Quinn

Cover Art by *Kim Mendoza*

The Wild Rose Press, Inc.
PO Box 708
Adams Basin, NY 14410-0708
Visit us at www.thewildrosepress.com

Publishing History
First Champagne Rose Edition, 2018
Print ISBN 978-1-5092-2264-3
Digital ISBN 978-1-5092-2265-0

Sycamore River Series
Published in the United States of America

Dedication

For Cecilia Christine Grassi,
my beloved first granddaughter,
a trailblazer, a maverick,
a girl born to dance and destined to soar.

Happy Reading!
M. Kate Quinn

Chapter One

Rylee MacDermott dragged the point of a box cutter along the seam of a storage carton, spread the flaps open, and stared at the shipment of lacy garters. Yup, she'd done it again. Slit the top one right in half as if she'd meant to.

"Un-freakin'-believable." She kicked the carton.

"Honestly, girl, must you talk like that?" Rosie Mandanello, Rylee's grandmother and owner extraordinaire of Rosie's Bridals, clucked her tongue. "It's your birthday. Be happy."

No easy task being happy to turn thirty when life was a shit show. Getting evicted from her apartment was a nice way to start her week. She'd had a gut feeling about her roommate from the get-go, so it should have been no surprise when Melanie, a blue-haired girl who had enough studs pierced to her face to throw off a metal detector had pocketed six months' worth of rent payments and disappeared, taking Rylee's too-expensive turbo-charged blender with her. She hadn't used the smoothie-making machine much, but still.

Now it was back to her mother and stepfather's house, back to her childhood bedroom where Paula Abdul was forever her girl in a giant poster on the wall. The image had been a teenage strategy of inspiration to stop eating peanut M&M's at night before bed, a habit she did not break then or now.

Was it too much to ask for things to fall into place for once? Freddie, her quote, unquote boyfriend, popped into her head. Bless his struggling-musician heart, Freddie had offered to move her into his place, share the expenses and cabinet space, which, of course, meant *share life*. Be a couple. A solution, yes, but something told her the prospect of moving in with a guy shouldn't make her feel like waiting for her turn at the dentist's office.

She appreciated Freddie and his one-bedroom walk-up across town. Her biggest problem with him, aside from his crazy-musician schedule of always working weekends and their dates usually amounting to her sitting alone at a café table listening to him play acoustic guitar during his coffeehouse gigs, was that she just didn't feel the *zoom*.

Her closest friend, Kit, the best seamstress on the planet and a big reason why Rylee's working at her grandmother's bridal shop didn't seem so lame, always laughed at her reference to the *zoom*. At the moment Kit was perched at her desk in the workroom of the bridal salon, hand-stitching delicate crystal beading on an illusion neckline of a client's gown. She smiled as if there was no tedium in the task, it maybe even giving her a little *zoom*.

Maybe she was idealistic to buy into the existence of the *zoom*, the chemical explosion between two people, the whoosh to your insides like an express-elevator ride from lobby to penthouse, that was the divining rod of all things relationship. But Rylee did. Granted, she'd watched a lot of old romantic movies with Rosie over the years, and despite her very good real-life reasons for skepticism, Rylee believed. And the fact was she and Freddie didn't have *zoom*.

Which didn't help that tonight Freddie was taking her for a birthday dinner to Rob's Steak House, the most expensive place in Sycamore River, where entrees cost as much as a cell phone payment. And for sure, he was going to bring up her moving in. She just knew it. And a big fat no waited in the back of her mouth like a canker sore oozing for release.

She strode across the wide-planked floor of the shop, put the box cutter back in its box, and flipped the latch. "You can't trust me with sharp objects, Rosie," she said. "I ruined another garter. This time I mean it. Take it out of my paycheck."

"Nonsense." Her grandmother waved a hand.

Rylee sighed. This was pity employment, although nobody would admit it, especially Rosie. Turning thirty just made it all the more humiliating to be back working at Rosie's Bridals, as she'd been doing off and on all her life since age fifteen. At her age it sucked to be her grandma's glorified clerk who regularly ruined merchandise.

Rosie, in her favorite sweater with the big pockets and the appliquéd rosebuds along the edges, came over to Rylee and pointed her letter opener at her like a weapon.

"Listen, you," she said in all her octogenarian feistiness. "Snap out of it, would you? You're giving me *agita*."

With two fingers, Rylee held up the sliced-in-two garter. "The churning acid in your belly aside, grandmother of mine, if you wanted to kick me to the curb I'd understand. It's not your job to provide me with employment anytime I get fired."

"Are you talking about that damn poodle again?"

"I got fired from dog walking." A caustic laugh popped out of her mouth. "You tell me who does that besides me?"

She'd tried her hand at dog walking when the opportunity presented itself on the bulletin board at the Shop-Rite. Who knew that walking somebody's pet could be that tricky? Yes, she'd underestimated the strength of a standard poodle, and yes, there were a few minutes when she couldn't exactly find dear Snowball, but it had all turned out okay. Snowball wound up fine, dirty and her coat matted with pine needles but unharmed after a romp near the river, and when Rylee had to cough up the money for a new grooming session that cost more than a day at the spa, if Rylee even knew what that might cost, that little job had set her back even further. So here she was back at Rosie Bridals, tearing garters to shreds. Nice.

"Kit"—Rosie pointed her pearl-handled weapon at her seamstress—"talk to your friend here before I give her a poke."

Kit, her long black hair piled on her head in a sloppy knot, reading glasses low on her nose, looked up from her handiwork. A crooked smile claimed her mouth. "Okay, let's see. New topic. What are you planning to wear tonight to dinner with Freddie?"

"I'm more concerned with how to tell him I don't want to be his roommate."

"Be sure about that before you turn the boy down." Rosie was back at her desk, slicing through a stack of mail, her spotty hands adept in the task. "Nice guys don't grow on trees, you know."

"Uh-oh." Kit lowered her head to her beads and thread.

"I know that, Gram." Rylee blew out a lungful of air. "But you and Grandpa Sal were the Barbie and Ken of your generation. Everybody envied your relationship, so you speak from a very high place, Rosie, my love."

"Oh, stop." Rosie waved a hand. "You're the one who put us on that pedestal. We were a normal couple who fought and made up and got on each other's nerves and loved each other no matter what. We weren't made by Mattel. Maybe you need to get your head out of the clouds."

"Let me ask you. When Grandpa Sal kissed you, did you get that *zooming* feeling inside here?" Rylee pointed to her chest.

Rosie took off her rhinestone-trimmed glasses, and her gray eyes twinkled with a hint of youth. "To his dying day."

"I rest my case."

"So what are you going to do, then? Break up with the guy because you're not *zooming?*" Rosie shook her head, tight gray curls unmoving. "You want to *zoom?* Ride a roller coaster."

"I don't want to stop seeing him. I mean, Freddie's nice, cute and all with that dimple in his chin and everything, and who doesn't like a guy who can play guitar, right? I just don't feel like *that* about him. So fingers crossed he doesn't put pressure on me."

Kit's mouth twisted into a bunch. "You think he will?"

"I just have a feeling about tonight. It's not going to go well."

5

Chapter Two

Darius Wirth sat across the mahogany table from his senior producer, Jake Richards, who in his custom-made shirt with the french cuffs, fidgeted, his gold links tapping a staccato against the wooden surface. The rest of the production team for their syndicated TV show, *Wirth More,* filed into the room and took their seats. The typical morning chitchat was absent today. This was a weighty meeting, and the tension in the air was electric, crackling.

With one more episode left to film for his business-rescue-themed reality show, they still hadn't found an ideal candidate for the finale. The show assisted floundering businesses, either those that were trying to get off the ground or those that, for whatever reason, had taken a downturn or stalled in their success.

Wirth More received some decent reviews during this first season, and the whole team hoped for renewal, but word was that their main sponsor, Parker Paper, was grumbling. If they pulled out, the gig was all over. That look on Jake's face this morning was testament.

Even though he and Jake were friends going back to their college days at Rutgers where they'd been roomies and fierce competitors when it came to grades and club football and girls, he hadn't given Darius a hint about today. That was how Jake operated. He liked being the only one in the know. Gave him power. It was annoying, but Jake had been the brainchild of the show and had lobbied for Darius to come on board as its host. So no complaints. But today Darius's stomach churned with anticipation.

"Okay, so," Jake began. "I got a heads-up from that chick Jennifer at Parker Paper. Tomorrow when we meet with the suits, they're going to chastise us about the choices we made in the previous eight episodes."

"Chastise? Why?" Emma, the station manager, looked up from her tablet. "*Wirth More* came in fifth in its timeslot for the week. Not stellar, granted, but still not bad."

"Yeah, but how did we compare to the other shows in Living Loud's lineup?" Darius asked. "We had to do better than that inane show with the two old ladies who make soup."

Jake laughed. "*Two Crocks* does better than you'd think. People love soup. Who knew?"

"I'd like to see the numbers." Darius liked working with numbers, the one thing his accounting degree had cemented into his brain. They could debate plenty when it came to the viability of their show. But the numbers were the numbers, and even if it could be that they sucked, at least they were accurate, true, real.

"According to Jennifer at Parker Paper—she wants me, by the way, so be grateful your producer is irresistible—the feedback is that they love the concept of the show, but there's a problem with the types of businesses we've worked with. Too male."

"Too male." It wasn't a question. Darius just felt the need to repeat the absurd comment.

"Dar, think about the shows we filmed. Bicycle shop, fly-fishing store, dry cleaner, pizzeria run by three brothers, small-engine repair, a printing place, and a leather guy."

"But, Jake, when we pitched Parker, their main concern was the thirty-to-forty-year-old demographic. We didn't pitch gender. And we've stuck to the plan. Each one of these businesses is operated by Generation Xers."

"Yeah, well, they're squawking. They say their main consumer is women, from the millennials to the baby boomers and beyond. Their products, paper towels, toilet paper, tissues, all that stuff, speak to women. Until now our episodes have spoken to men. That has to change. And it has to change now. They won't agree to a second season, even with our decent numbers, until we guarantee we'll select businesses that will appeal more to the female audience."

Darius pulled in a breath in order to unlock his chest. "So what's going down tomorrow when we meet with them? Did your 'girlfriend' tell you that too?"

Jake snorted, clearly loving that he had a leg up due to his so-called charm. "Let's put it this way, Darius. When your main sponsor threatens to pull the plug, you play their way unless you want to be out of a job. And none of us wants that, do we?" He wagged a finger. "How're you supposed to pay for that waterfront pad of yours in Hoboken, huh, Darius? We do what our sponsor asks, that's how."

His place on the river had been a pricey purchase. It was also fact that he and Jake had vied against each other in a silent bidding war on the prime two-bed, two-bath unit with balcony. But when they'd learned they had been bidding for the same property, the old rivalry accelerated. Jake did not lose well—that was for sure—

so he took every opportunity to throw it up in Darius's face that his place had cost a lung.

Darius had paid more money than he'd wanted, had gotten wrapped up in the competition. No way would he admit just how much he needed Parker Paper to remain in place as the show's main sponsor. Losing his job would be ugly.

"Darius, we need to work our magic, okay, buddy? We've got to tell Parker Paper we've found a female-friendly business to use as our final episode of the season. After it airs, if the numbers indicate that more women are tuning in, they'll sign on for season two."

Darius scanned the faces around the table, all eyes on him. "Okay. I'll pull an all-nighter searching the internet. Believe me—I'll come up with something."

His cell phone sounded, and he muttered an expletive but was quick to connect the call from The Memory Center, the facility in his hometown of Sycamore River, where his father lived.

Toni, the woman who handled the finances at the top-notch Alzheimer's facility, chirped in his ear. Just hearing her birdlike voice brought back the agonizing finagling it had taken to arrange for Pop to become a resident.

"Is my father okay?"

"Yes," the voice chirped. "No changes. But there is an issue we'd like to discuss with you. Would you be able to come out and meet with me?"

"What's this about?"

"It's a financial matter. When can you meet with me?"

He looked at his watch. The train trek to Sycamore River from Hoboken was only forty-five minutes. "I'll be there at four o'clock. That okay?"

"See you then."

Jake's gaze was locked on him. "Everything okay with your father?" His ability to make himself sound concerned was impressive. The only thing the man really cared about was money.

"I've got to head over to the nursing home for a meeting."

"Don't let it eat up your whole night, Darius. You've got work to do."

This was going to be a long one.

Chapter Three

When he came to pick her up, Freddie wore new jeans and he might have even run an iron over his button-down shirt. This was not good. Instead of his normal fleece-lined denim jacket, he wore an oversized black woolen coat. The look was almost formal for a guy like Freddie. And that made it all the worse for Rylee to let the poor guy down. Her stomach was a tangled knot, as if her guts were doing a cat's cradle.

"You look really nice." His appreciative smile was another indication that this was a serious night and not at all just a Saturday grabbing a burger at Jabberwocky's downtown pub. Freddie was usually oblivious to what she wore, certainly didn't dole out compliments. Bad, bad.

Rylee smoothed a hand down the green blouse, a gift from her mother. The silkiness of the fabric was too flimsy for wintertime, and she'd have much preferred wearing a cable-knit sweater. But when her mother had painted on that pout of hers and asked why she wasn't wearing the blouse, Rylee plucked it from the gift bag and cut the tags. Besides the gooseflesh that was already marching along her bare arms, she worried the pretty blouse coupled with her cute black skirt could send Freddie a mixed message.

"Thanks." She produced a smile and quickly shrugged into her long black woolen coat, buttoning up to the neck. "Um, you too."

"Cool purse."

It was a birthday gift from Rosie, a too-tiny, can't-fit-anything-in-it, long-handled clutch. But just looking at the girly, red patent-leather thing with its ridiculously large bow made her grin. So Rosie. "Makes you swanky," Rosie had said when she'd given it to her.

She stepped out into the night air and pulled in a deep breath, the cold stinging her lungs. She was ready. Tonight she'd have "the talk" with Freddie over drinks and dinner to mark her thirtieth birthday. The timing was right. She'd tell him that before she could move in with anyone, she had to first live alone, establish herself. The plan made all the sense in the world.

At Rob's Steak House they checked their nearly matching black woolen dress coats, and Freddie slipped the numbered tag into his shirt pocket.

When they'd been seated in the dark, ornate dining room, a middle-aged lady named Margaret delivered their drinks. Rylee worried the linen napkin she held between her hands under the table. *Where to begin?*

"So"—Freddie lifted his glass—"let's toast."

"Okay." Her guts crocheted themselves into a doily.

"To you, Rylee." He tapped his glass against her wine goblet.

She took a tiny sip. The merlot was delicious, fruity, and pungent. She'd savor it.

Freddie tipped his head in contemplation, his eyes kind of googly. To hell with a ladylike sip. She guzzled the merlot.

"You're a great girl."

Another gulp of her drink, as if it were fruit punch

and not a fine wine. "Freddie," she began just as Margaret came up to their table and asked if they were ready to order.

Freddie told her they hadn't looked at the menu yet, and when she retreated, his eyes zeroed in on Rylee again. She swigged from her goblet.

He reached across the table with one open palm. "Give me your hand."

Her chest locked. What was he up to? She slid her right hand across the starchy tablecloth, just in case he went insane and had something to slip onto a finger of her left hand. He took her hand and closed his fingers around hers. His hand was clammy, like cold cuts.

"You know how much I care about you, Rylee," he said, all tenderness and sincerity yet, sadly, *zoom* free.

She cleared her throat. "Freddie, there's something—"

"I'm moving to LA."

Her heart stalled in her chest and then did a kind of whirligig. "Did you say you're moving to California?"

"Yes." He squeezed her hand with that half-a-pound-of-boiled-ham paw of his. She tugged free. "I know this sounds kind of out of left field." He uttered a sheepish chuckle. "But I've had it in the back of my mind for a while now."

"You mean all this time when you were asking me to move in with you? How did that fit into your plan? I'm confused."

"Rylee." He shook his head and looked up at the ceiling before he met her gaze. "I'm so sorry. Did you think I was asking you to move in with me, like as a couple?"

"Yes, of course. That's what you said."

"No, no, no." He shook his head as if there were a bee in his hair. "It was a business deal. I'm sorry you misunderstood. I've got eight months left on my lease, and Gerry's going to take it over but needed a roommate. I thought of you immediately when you lost your apartment."

"Gerry? You actually thought I'd enjoy living with Gerry?" A vision of Freddie's bass player came to mind. Gerry, in his black socks and Birkenstocks even in wintertime, his grizzly head of hair that hadn't seen shampoo in ages, his breath that would definitely wilt her African violets, her roommate? "You wanted me to cohabitate with a Neanderthal?"

"He's a good guy." Freddie's mouth quirked in a half grin. "Give you the shirt off his back. As a matter of fact, that's his coat I wore tonight."

"He doesn't bathe."

Freddie emitted a whoop of laughter. "Maybe you could have been a good influence on him. And you'd have loved Bonnie and Clyde."

"Who are Bonnie and Clyde?"

"His Maine coon cats. Brother and sister. They're no trouble at all. Hairy, though."

"I'm allergic to cats, Freddie." She blew out air. "Welts. I get welts the size of silver dollars."

"Really? Wow. That's pretty big."

"I don't understand. You and I were going along fine dating. Things were good—you know, decent— and now you're moving to California and when it came to me, all you thought of was your apartment?"

"Well, you're the one who said you couldn't stand that you had to move in with your parents. I figured it could have been a win-win. See?"

"No, Freddie, actually, I don't see. You should have let me know all sides of that deal when you made the offer. You should have told me that your ultimate goal was to move to California to, what, become a famous musician?"

"You sound angry."

"Not angry. Just surprised. I feel like you tried to pull one over on me."

He shook his head slowly this time, as if he were oh so sad, and suddenly Rylee thought he might be a shyster disguised as an unassuming, dimple-chinned struggling artist. "Not at all, Rylee. That's not my style. Look, let's just cut our losses, huh, babe? I mean, we had fun, right?"

She was speechless. All she could do was guzzle merlot. She watched him over the rim of her goblet. Who was he?

"Oh." He pulled his mouth into a rectangle. "By the way, I found somebody for the apartment, so that's not an option now. Sorry." He let the rectangle of his mouth snap back into a kind of solicitous curve that begged for a punch. "But you'll find something."

"I have some stuff at your place I'll need to collect."

"Already thought of it," he said with pride, as if he'd studied for a quiz. "I put it all in a bag. It's in my car. Your pajamas, the box of tampons, body wash, your floss, everything."

"I see. How handy." She drained the rest of the wine and placed the goblet onto the linen tablecloth. "When do you leave?"

"We have a flight out of Newark on Monday."

Did he say *we*? "Who's going with you? Johnny?

Ray?" Those were the other guys he played with, the keyboardist and the drummer.

"Abigail."

"The redhead who plays the triangle?" Rylee let out a scoffing sound and didn't care about the heads that turned at the table next to theirs. Abigail with the tattoo on her leg of the leprechaun guy from the cereal box? She snorted again. Maybe Abigail was magically delicious. "Does she think she's going to tap a triangle into fame and fortune out in California?"

"No," he said with an exaggerated pout and a knit brow, a countenance of contrition. With that face, he could be in a confessional booth right now. "We sort of fell in love."

In her heart of hearts, she didn't care if Freddie fell in love with Abigail, the magically delicious triangle banger. She really did not. What did matter was that this was another one of her lose-lose situations. Did she ever learn? Apparently not. She did not see a hint of this coming. And here she'd been afraid of hurting him, had been concerned that he was going to propose, and meanwhile her tampons and dental floss were waiting for her in his car. Freddie wasn't the joke. She was.

She threw the linen napkin onto the table and grabbed her purse. "Well, I think this evening is over." She gave him an open palm. "Let me have the tag for my coat."

"I'm sorry." He fished the cardboard disk from his pocket.

She couldn't give him the reprieve. No, she would not tell him it was okay. She was sick to the point of puke with telling people it was okay. *Go to LA with Abigail and be happy. Live on love, whatever.* "Good luck," she did manage to say. "I hope it turns out the way you plan."

She turned on her heel and went to the coat check before he could mutter another gratuitous sound. She pulled out her phone and hit the app for the new driver service, EZridr, a simple swipe of her finger summoning a ride, indicating the destination, and making a payment all in one.

The car arrived in record time, and she dashed to it. With the door open, she heard his voice behind her. "Rylee," he called. "Don't forget the bag with your stuff." He thrust a handled brown paper bag at her.

She yanked the bag, tearing off one side of the handle. She jumped into the car and slammed the door.

****

In the back seat of the SUV, swallowed in the big heavy coat, her purse strap slung across her body cadet-like, she clutched the damn paper page of her belongings. She seethed.

Then she sneezed. She sneezed again. Three more times. She started to itch, her neck, her hands, her torso. She lifted her arms, and her heart sank. This coat had no cuffs. Hers did. She reached into the pockets and pulled out a half-eaten Twix bar and a condom packet. *Shoot me.* The attendant had given her the wrong damn coat. She was wearing Gerry's coat of germs that had to be covered in cat hair. Thank you, Bonnie and Clyde.

She had to get out of this thing. She wrestled first with the purse's strap, which somehow was tangled with the seat belt. She tugged and pulled and nearly choked herself in the effort. She coughed and sneezed again. The SUV twisted and turned along the roadways, and she fought to stay upright as she tugged at Gerry's fleabag of a coat.

"You okay back there?" The driver's big eyes stared at her from the rearview mirror.

"Yes, I'm fine." She sneezed and scratched at her skin while she gyrated around the back seat.

She continued a kind of calisthenics in freeing herself from the coat of death. Finally, as planned, the driver brought her to Maple Avenue in downtown Sycamore River, right in front of Jo-Jo's Java House where she'd planned to bide some time and sip a coffee concoction to avoid a barrage of questions from her mother and stepfather that returning at this early hour would cause.

Before the driver had even put the vehicle in park, Rylee opened the door and threw out the hairball of a coat. She missed a mesh garbage pail by a mile. This birthday sucked. This night could not get any worse.

Chapter Four

Darius was late, very late. But because The Memory Center took such a personal interest in its residents, they were even willing to accommodate his crazy schedule. The woman, Toni, was waiting for him to get there, even though it would be beyond six p.m. when he'd finally arrived.

As the train pulled into the station, self-reproach churned in his belly. Here it was mid-January and he hadn't been to see Pop since Christmas. Sycamore River wasn't across the continent. The only excuse he had was that he wanted so much for his show to be a success and get picked up for a second season that he'd put all his time there. When it came down to it, *Wirth More* was worth most. He was a shitty son, even if Pop rarely even knew he was there whenever he did visit. He should be there.

He was reminded of Christmas, how he'd stood at the old man's bed with a gift of new flannel pajamas and slippers and Pop had stared at him with those cloudy blue eyes absent of any recognition. A garish grin broke across the old man's face.

"Happy birthday," Pop proffered a gravelly attempt of joviality. "Is it my birthday again?"

"No, Pop. It's Christmas. Merry Christmas." Darius put the packages on the end of the bed. "These are for you."

19

His father pulled the shoebox into his tentative grasp, and his bumpy arthritic fingers fought with the paper.

"Need some help?" Darius stood beside the bed, feeling helpless.

Pop looked up from his task. "So how old are you, boy?"

"Me? Pop, I'm thirty-five."

"Well, happy birthday, then. Where's your mother? She should be here. Hey." Pop's face had taken on a clownish gleam. "Did I ever tell you how your mother and I met?"

A smile slanted Darius's mouth now as he pressed his head back against the train seat, hoping the steady vibration of the car rumbling over the tracks might lull him for a few minutes, give him a chance to regroup.

Amazingly, it happened every time he visited his father. The story of how his old man had won the heart of Arabella, his wife of forty years. When Mom died from a ruptured aortic aneurysm five years ago on her way to the hospital, Darius swore his father's mental decline began that very day. In a way he'd lost them both in one shot.

It had started with simple things. Telling the same story over and over again, that coup of how he'd convinced the young Spanish beauty Arabella Vega to marry him by surprising her with the oil painting that cost him his 1970 Pacemaker fishing boat with the twin diesel engines. On and on, Pop told the tale, laughing at how his Arabella jumped for joy and accepted his proposal, not caring one iota that his rigid parents didn't like her because she was Spanish and her disapproving parents doubted the future she'd have with a struggling electrician.

Mitchell Wirth had won his bride, and when he reiterated the tale, even now his eyes shone like the old days, the clouds in them breaking way for the light that flashed again, if only for a single moment. Nowadays Darius didn't mind his father's droning on and on simply for the glimpse of life that came to his eyes.

His mind played a series of clips of the stuff that had pushed him to seek a nursing home for his father. The forgetting to pay a bill, not remembering to eat lunch or dinner, forgetting to bathe or change out of his pajamas were all problems with Darius in Hoboken and Pop in Sycamore River. The going back and forth had been tough. He'd hoped hiring someone to check up on Pop on a daily basis would have bought them some time, but the old guy's decline had come swiftly. Finally, when he almost burned his house down by trying to start some logs in the fireplace, which was electric and not wood burning, Darius investigated nursing homes.

The Memory Center, located just north of Sycamore River and set on acres of rolling knolls rimmed with tall sturdy pines, had all the qualifications and was his top pick. It cost a fortune, but with selling the house and the pension from the electrical union combined with his social security checks, Pop had an opportunity to live in the best facility New Jersey had to offer for the aged with all stages of memory loss.

And now they wanted a briefing. The work he needed to do on prospects for the show would have to wait. Right now, his mind was on his father and The Memory Center.

****

The cab from the train station dropped him off in the front of the old mansion that had been converted into the nursing home back in the nineties. Previously, the place had belonged to a former governor's daughter who bequeathed the dwelling and grounds to the memory foundation, as their family had suffered the ills of Alzheimer's and dementia.

Inside the marble entry, Darius went to the left where double doors led to the main office. He figured the room may have originally been the parlor, and although at one time the space may have been a place of easy conversation and visiting, he was sure no such activity would happen here in this space today. Something was wrong. He didn't know exactly what, but he was about to find out.

Toni, a small and spry woman, ushered him into an office where he sat in a maroon leather side chair and waited. He eyed the place. He'd been in this room before. This was where he'd come to discuss having Pop take residence. The administrators had been very nice, accommodating. The facility was small and personal, and he'd been satisfied that it was the right place for his father to live in comfort and receive the proper care for the time he had left.

Sam Gerard, the head of the finance department, entered the room, his short, square body clothed in a dark gray suit that fit him well. Darius wished he had dressed more formally, looking down at his jeans—his good jeans, but still—and his leather bomber jacket.

"Thank you for coming," Sam said.

"What's this about? Is everything okay with my father?"

"His doctors say he's doing as well as possible at

this point, Darius. I'm sure they've discussed with you what to expect."

Darius nodded, fighting to file away the ugly news of those expectations.

Sam flipped open a file folder that sat on his desk blotter. "There is a problem, Darius, that I hope we'll resolve in the best way possible." He pinned Darius with his gaze. "Your father's funds have run low, and with his monthly contributions, it's just not going to be enough for him to stay with us."

It was as if the floor had fallen away and Darius floated through space. How could the three hundred thousand dollars that came from the sale of his parents' house be all but gone already? What about Dad's stock portfolio? The bonds he'd cashed in? "That can't be." He had had the cost all figured out. He was a numbers guy, damn it. "We had this conversation when my father arrived. I was assured we were set for a good while."

Sam removed his glasses. He rubbed his eyes with a pinch of his thumb and index finger. "I know. But it has been three years, and, well, a premier facility is costly. Your father doesn't have long-term-care insurance, and as you know, he wasn't able to recoup as much from his portfolio as he hoped due to the stock market's unpredictability. I'm very sorry, Darius. But we're determined to help your father transition somewhere else that will both meet his needs and be within his financial capability."

"What's that mean? Are there other places as good as this one?"

"Well, you can't compare apples and oranges, but there are adequate facilities."

"Adequate." The word tasted like paint in his mouth. "Are you talking about state-run places?"

Sam offered a short nod, kept a poker face. "Don't be scared off by the sound of that. We'll help you sort through the options, Darius. Toni's gone for the day now, so let's see if I can get into the calendar program to set up an appointment for you as soon as tomorrow, if that works for you." He turned his attention to his computer screen and tapped with two fingers at the keyboard.

"How about Thursday? I'm in meetings all day tomorrow." He was scheduled to meet with Parker Paper tomorrow.

Sam scanned the screen. "I'm afraid not. Friday works, though. How about Friday, late afternoon?"

Darius's mind was a jumble of thoughts. Whatever was going on with *Wirth More,* he had to settle this situation with his father. "Yes, Friday. I'll be here."

He had no choice. Getting his father into this place had been nothing short of a miracle when the need came. There was always a waiting list, and the gruesome fact was that available beds didn't happen because a resident decided to move on to Hawaii or Tahiti. Somebody had to up and die for another to be received. Everything about this stunk like yesterday's garbage.

He liked this place. Pop liked this place. For maybe the first time in his life, he and his father were on the same page about something. All those wasted years of avoiding each other because, frankly, they had gotten on each other's nerves since way back when, and now there was a peace between them whenever Darius visited. This ugly disease and whatever medications that came with it had taken away Mitchell Wirth's strict edge. It sucked that it had taken just about everything else as well.

He thought of his father, up on the third floor in the bed by the window, a coveted spot, wearing his too-big pajamas, what was left of his hair puffing out around his head like cotton. This was not the old man who had locked him out of the house so many times Darius couldn't count. This wasn't the Mitchell Wirth who accused him of never amounting to anything and of being a disappointment when he changed majors in college, deciding on a career path in communications.

"Communications," his father had bellowed with incredulity, as if Darius had announced he'd chosen to be a circus clown. "How's a job like that supposed to buy groceries and pay rent?" But this old man, in his brittle body and craggy face, had no fight in him. Worse, he was at the mercy of his only son, the son who had thrown away a good opportunity to become an accountant for some pie-in-the-sky job in communications, and that sucked even more. It came down to numbers, and Darius had dropped the ball. He hated this. Everywhere he turned was in flux.

"Darius," Sam interrupted his zigzagging thoughts. "You okay?"

"I'm still trying to process this stuff."

Sam gave a sympathetic nod. "This, unfortunately, can happen when patients outlive their funds. I'm sorry."

"How much for my father to be able to stay here?"

"Darius, truly, we'll be able to fin—"

"How much?" He hadn't meant to sound angry. This guy hadn't done anything but try to help. "Sorry, man. I know you're trying to remedy the situation, but I do need to know what we're dealing with here."

"One hundred thousand."

Trying not to flinch, Darius kept his eyes on the man. "Okay. And that's for how long?"

"Up to one year."

Was the guy telling him that was all the time he believed Pop had left in him? This conversation made his skin crawl. There was no way in hell Darius could cough up a hundred grand, especially now that his TV show could very well be on the chopping block. He might be out on his ass himself. How cruel to think that his college tuition had cost his parents nearly as much as his father needed now to live in this good facility. Pop's residence could come down to one last quintessential disappointment from his son. Fate was cruel.

Would that man up there, who spent his days staring out his window with vacant eyes, even know what was going on? Would it matter to him one way or the other where? Darius suspected that somewhere deep inside, the old guy would know, and just like the old Mitchell who showed up whenever he told the tale of how he'd won the hand of Arabella Vega, he'd realize his kid had let him down.

He took a deep breath and exhaled. "I can't come up with that kind of money."

The man nodded with a downward turn to his mouth. "Not too many people can."

"I guess I'll see what options there are."

On the way out of the office, Darius passed a neat stack of the local newspapers on a small table. He plucked up a copy of what promised to be a good dose

26

of distraction and tucked it under his arm. Then he headed to his favorite place, Jo-Jo's Java House on Maple Avenue, for a hot cup of the Jamaican blend.

Chapter Five

When Rylee attempted to step from the vehicle, the EZridr driver warned her to watch out for the slush. She cursed Freddie. She wore her best black leather boots, and if they got ruined in a slush puddle, well, it would be his goddamn fault.

She stepped gingerly from the vehicle, and the frigid air assaulted her face and her bare arms and legs. What the hell was she doing in an outfit like this on this wicked-cold night? An arctic wind slammed against her and flooded her bones.

Her gaze scanned the sidewalk. Somehow the cat-fur-riddled wrong coat she'd torpedoed from the SUV's window had missed the slushiness on the sidewalk and sat in a lump under the protruding eave of the storefront next to Jo-Jo's. It was an impressive distance. Those days of high school softball had paid off after all.

She almost made it over the river of icy, muddy gook that ran along the curb of Maple Avenue, but when her foot came down onto the sidewalk, it landed sideways, and she tripped, almost fell over, righted herself by swinging her arms, but had turned her ankle. She winced, muttered a favorite expletive, limped over to the coat, grabbed it up from the cold cement, and shrugged back into it. She ignored the eyes of a group of college kids standing nearby and tamped down the urge to salute them with one cold digit. Then she hobbled up to Jo-Jo's Java House.

She ordered herself a large macchiato, a birthday splurge both in moolah and calories, and she savored her first decadent sip off the top, disturbing the delicate crosshatch design of the espresso in the frothy milk. The expertly prepared beverage was the best part of her night, worth more than every cent in her purse. Her breath locked in her chest. She knew without looking what was in that ridiculous-looking purse—her phone and a lipstick. *Un-freakin'-believable!*

The remaining handle of the brown paper bag filled with toiletries tore away, and the bag fell with a thud, the contents spilling over the coffeehouse floor. She scrambled to gather her belongings, feeling the eyes of patrons from where they sat at bistro tables or from where they stood in line behind her. Would a fistful of tampons be considered legal tender? Crap with a capital C. She shoved them into her purse and stuffed the rest of her items into the deep pockets of the fleabag coat, even the plaid boxers with the big yellow smiley face emblazed across the ass that she'd worn for bed.

She looked up into the quizzical gaze of the young guy behind the counter. "Oh boy." She produced a smile. "I, uh, I'm embarrassed to say I don't have my wallet."

The barista she knew from the day shift whenever she had come in to get her and Rosie cups of coffee was not here tonight. This guy had that sucks-to-be-you look on his face when she told him she couldn't pay for the coffee.

"Uh, here's the thing"—she leaned in to read his nameplate—"Corey. I'm good for it, honestly. I'm here all the time. I work with my grandmother, Rosie

29

Mandanello, who owns Rosie's Bridals on Main Street. Do you know it?" Corey just stared at her. "I usually order from Nico. Do you know Nico?"

"Yeah. He's not here."

Rylee cleared her throat. "Yes, I see that." She took her purse's clasp between two fingers and twisted it open. She withdrew her phone. "Okay, look. I'll just make a quick phone call…" Casting her gaze down to the device's screen, she saw it was black. She swiped a frantic finger across the blank face. Nothing. She swiped again, knowing it was as dead as a doornail. She looked back up at the guy. "I, uh, forgot to charge it." No response. "How about this, uh, Corey? What if I write down my name and number and I promise to come back in the morning to pay you?"

"That's not really allowed. I'm pretty sure." He shrugged. "I'm new."

"Uh-huh, right. Okay, well, do you have a supervisor here I could talk to?"

"I'm the supervisor."

"Oh." Were supervisor's twelve years old these days, because that was just about how old this kid looked? And nice, she couldn't even walk a poodle from point A to point B without screwing that up.

"Maybe I can help."

Rylee turned to the voice behind her, and her gaze fell upon a dark-haired, dark-eyed man in a leather bomber jacket, and just like that, her stomach went from penthouse to lobby. *Zoom*. She couldn't pull her attention away from his onyx eyes, nor could she prevent the sudden slackness of her jaw. He wasn't tremendously tall or perfectly handsome in that movie-star kind of way or anything. Truthfully, he had a crooked kind of nose, as if he'd broken it sometime, maybe in a scuffle with someone. He looked like the type of guy who had scuffled when he was a teenager. A bad boy, she'd bet money. But she didn't have any goddamn money. And of all times. She was mortified that this man with the black hair that shone blue under the lights of Jo-Jo's Java House had to have heard the conversation with Corey, the Doogie Howser of baristas.

"How much do you need?" He sounded irritated, although because of his appeal, she was prone to give him the benefit of the doubt. Maybe it was just her imagination. She tended to project. She was pissed off tonight with all that went on and couldn't even begin to imagine what she must look like right about now. So maybe she was the only pissed-off one here at Jo-Jo's. Well, she and Corey.

"Look, lady, there's a line behind you." Corey pointed a finger, but she didn't turn to see. What good would it do?

The guy with the decent, no, nice and interesting face inclined his head toward the barista. As he got closer, she took in a scent of pine. She liked pine.

"I've got her coffee. What do I owe you?"

"The extra large is four twenty-eight with tax, and the extra caramel sauce is fifty cents more. So four seventy-eight."

There it was. His inky eyes flashed with a statement like a headline in the newspaper. Accusation shone bright. That along with the side slant of his mouth she knew what he was thinking. Yeah, that uber-expensive coffee was a tall order for someone who had no money on her, but none of this was her fault. She wasn't a thief. Suddenly, *zoom* or no *zoom*, she didn't like this guy. She wished he'd just say it so she could snap back at him. She needed to snap at somebody about something. Mr. Big Shot over here with his piney smell, acting all condescending going to step in and save the day. No and more no. She was officially thirty years old. Today was her birthday, and she would be nobody's damsel ever again if it killed her or landed her in the pokey.

Rylee turned to Corey again, and her look implored him. "Do not take this man's money."

"Well, I'm going to have to take somebody's money. What's it going to be?"

"I promise I'll bring the money to you tomorrow. First thing in the morning."

"Why don't you just let me buy the coffee? There's a line of people waiting, you know."

With his mouth twisted all stern like that, he looked like a pirate, black eyebrows tilting in on themselves, insolent shake of his head causing a shock of hair to fall over his forehead like Superman's. Hot, yes, but she didn't like him now.

Rylee peered around the pirate. Four people indeed waited in line behind him. "Sorry." She turned back to Corey. "Can I use your phone?" She felt like a total loser, an extremely cranky loser. She scratched at her neck. The damn coat was killing her.

"It's not allowed." The way Corey's mouth pulled downward at the corners, exposing his lower teeth, made her flinch. This guy found her pathetic or maybe he assumed she was homeless. Technically, she was, so that made it all the worse. Her face flamed.

"Maybe just this one time you can let me use the

phone to call someone?"

Corey folded his arms and shook his head.

"Miss." The pirate with the Superman hair stepped up beside her. He laid a five-dollar bill on the counter. "Enough already. You're being ridiculous."

"You're ridiculous," she said, which made no sense whatsoever unless you were a kindergartener on a playground. To make matters worse, this pirate with his big hand resting atop a five-spot smelled like the woods in autumn. She breathed him in while she wished he'd go away.

When he pushed the bill forward, she shoved it back toward him. Her action along with the swinging arm of the too-big coat caused the clasp of her girlie purse to come undone, and the stupid-looking red patent leather useless thing tipped over and looking like a slicked-red open mouth, spit tampons onto the floor.

She stood there, out-of-body-experience type of feeling, and looked at the splay of intimate supplies strewn on the floor like fat pickup sticks. Like a squirrel on crack, she gathered it all and shoved items into the deep pockets of Freddie's coat. The flurry of movement managed to stir up some of the allergens in the coat, and she began a string of sneezes.

"Lady, can't you see there's a ton of people waiting?" Corey motioned with his head. "Just let me take the guy's money, okay? Do us all a favor."

While she was trying to think of what to say next, a rush of conversation got her attention. That group of college-aged kids she'd seen outside had come into the store, boisterous and giddy in all their youthfulness, full of chitchat. Suddenly, she felt old—an old cat lady with no cat, just the fur. The line behind Rylee was now all the way to the door.

"What's the hold up?" one of the kids called from the back.

"Some lady has no money," someone responded. "She looks like she's on something."

"That's the same lady we saw outside."

"She's shoving stuff in her pockets. Maybe she robbed a pharmacy."

"Aw," said one of the girls in the bunch. "That's sad."

"Is she homeless? Let's buy her food."

"She's got to be homeless. Look at that coat. And there's clothing sticking out of a pocket."

"Aw," a girl said. "Poor lady."

Despite herself, Rylee's gaze slid to meet the pirate's gaze. His mouth—rather lush, she couldn't help but notice because she was a mouth person—twitched with what she decided was his effort not to laugh at her. A surge of heat climbed up her neck and flooded her face. She was a blusher, and she was sure her face was now neon. If a hole in the floor would just appear and swallow her up, she would count it as her best birthday present ever.

****

"Take the money." Darius didn't have any more time for this.

The woman met his gaze with defiance, eyes a combo green with a yellow inner circle around the pupils, eyes like a cat. Those cat eyes bore into him with disdain, as if instead of offering to buy her coffee, he were attempting to steal her purse. She glanced at the group of patrons who had assembled over the last few minutes.

"For God's sake," she groaned. "Fine, okay. Fine."

Her impertinence took him aback. What did she have against chivalry? She was an odd one with her cat eyes bright with fury she had no business to display and that chin she jutted up at him, ready for round one. He bit a tooth down onto his lower lip to stifle the laugh that threatened to escape. All he wanted to do was pay for her lavish drink so she'd get out of his way and allow him to order his own damn cup of damn coffee like everyone else in line simply waiting for this rabid woman to settle her damn bill.

Suddenly, the woman breathed a sigh and looked to Darius with eyes swimming. Was this display about something other than coffee? She opened her mouth to speak, but nothing came out. She closed the lips—full and pink, he noticed now. She sighed again. "Look, mister, I'm really not, you know, a homeless person or a crazy person or anything. I can pay for my own coffee. Usually. I, uh, appreciate you paying my tab, okay? I promise to pay you back. I just need to know how to get it to you."

"It's only a few dollars," he said. "My treat. How's that?"

"Nope, no treat. Do you have a business card or something?"

"Really…"

"Please." She pinned him with her gaze. "Please," she said again in a near whisper.

An odd tugging began somewhere in his chest, and he was quick to dismiss it with a little cough. He withdrew his wallet and handed her a business card.

She scanned the text. "Thank you, Darius Wirth. I'll mail you a check."

His instinct was to tell her again not to bother, but he didn't want to rile her again. Instead, he offered a shake of his head. "Okay, then."

As he was leaving, one of the college guys stepped in front of him. "Yo, mister, I recorded the whole thing in case there was a problem."

He gave the kid an incredulous look. "Seriously, there was no reason for that."

"Are you kidding? I thought she was going to start swinging." The kid smiled with pride. "You're that guy on the TV show that helps, like, stores that are almost belly up, right?"

He offered a smile but figured if he engaged these kids any longer, he'd never get out of Jo-Jo's. He cast his gaze to give the feisty woman another glance, but she was gone.

****

Rylee trudged from the coffee shop, the frigid air biting her face. She hoped it would help lower her blood pressure because she felt like a percolator ready to boil over. She was mad but not really sure where to direct the fierce feeling. That poor guy at the coffee shop, the young barista, Corey, with the scared-looking eyes, was probably traumatized for having had to deal with her.

And Darius—*who's named Darius anyway?*—with his pirate face and Superman hair, with that look in his black eyes. She'd felt a *zoom* when she was close to him, enough of a zap of heat in her veins to convince herself she wasn't crazy that such chemistry existed. Her chemistry was still popping like kernels of corn over an open flame. Such a dichotomy of feelings, wishing she'd never laid eyes on the guy because of the utter embarrassment of the situation, yet wanting to be near him again just to feel the popcorn popping in her bloodstream.

It was like that time when she'd ridden the biggest roller coaster at Six Flags, and the entire sixty seconds had been hell, and she'd chanted to herself during that too-long minute that she'd never ever get on that thing again. And when it was over she'd missed the rush so much, she got on the stupid ride again and screamed again and vowed again only to do it three more times. She was a glutton for her own punishment.

When she got to her mother and stepfather's house, she paused before going in. This was such a bad birthday. Thank God this night was over. She couldn't take another minute of it. With a deep breath, the vapor wafting out into the cold night, she plodded up the front steps and entered the house.

The lights were on in the living room, and her mother, Angie, sat on the sofa. Sonny, Rylee's favorite stepfather, was seated beside her, pressed so close they were squeezed onto one cushion. Her mother's eyes were glassy, foreign, staring. She fixed her gaze on Rylee.

"Mom?" Rylee's heart clicked in her chest. "What's going on?"

"Rosie's dead."

Chapter Six

On the train ride home, Darius was tempted not to answer the phone when he saw it was Jake calling, but with all that was going on with *Wirth More*, he had no choice.

"Jake, hi."

"Everything okay with your father?" Jake asked.

Darius didn't miss the tapping sound of Jake's fingers working his keyboard. The man's attention was really there, not with Pop's condition. He was a bullshit aficionado, but the guy was slick, and he was smart, and he was the boss.

"Eh." Darius leaned back in the seat and closed his eyes. "Might have to find a new facility. The one he's in is too much money."

"But you said you like that place, right? They play games with him and stuff, right?"

"Yeah, they do." One day he'd walked into his father's room to find two nursing assistants playing Uno with Pop, the two ladies perched at the end of his bed, the cards strewn across the bedclothes. They'd been doing their damnedest to get Pop to engage.

"In order for him to stay at the Memory Center, I'm going to have to win the lottery."

Jake snorted into Darius's ear. "Or find the ideal business for our show. Pronto."

"Yeah, or that."

****

Sipping from a water bottle, Darius gazed out his kitchen window. He was glad to be home. His was a corner unit, and being on the top floor, his terrace was the largest. This was one hell of a place, right at the water's edge, the vista of city and watercraft zipping over the Hudson, the water inky-black tonight, there for the viewing. He couldn't help but feel that satisfaction whenever the topic of this place came up with Jake. It burned his ass that Darius had bought it. But how was he supposed to know Jake was serious about the unit when it went up for sale? Even back to the days when the two friends had been roomies in college, Jake was always talking smack, offering up what his intentions were, and quite often it was all lip service. So Forty-Four Frank Sinatra Boulevard, the top floor, unit 6D, was the place Darius called home.

He stood at the granite counter and thought about the woman in Jo-Jo's Java House tonight. He tended to critique everything and everyone, categorizing his way through life. The woman at Jo-Jo's definitely went into the curious category. He was curious about her, and damned if he knew why. She wasn't all too remarkable looking except for her eyes, almond-shaped and fringed with long lashes. Cat eyes. She was medium height, and even in that shroud of a coat, he suspected she had some decent curves, not skinny by any means.

He hated skinny women with stick legs in their skintight denim leggings. He liked women with a little meat on them, some female contours. He attributed his penchant to his Spanish blood. His Spanish side liked curves. The woman had been disheveled with her dark brown hair askew and trailing down her back in a zigzag, as though she'd just gotten out of bed. But somehow he recognized something in her that pricked at his insides.

The large almond-shaped orbs the color of springtime were definitely feline. She was feline. What was it, though? Why, with all that he had to think about with the show and his father, did she occupy his mind tonight?

Maybe it was the way she'd said "please." Said it twice. As if she couldn't take one more thing to not go her way. He had an instinct about people, which made him so good at what he did. He was able to tell when a business was worth rescuing, when the owners had their heart in their establishment, and when they didn't. And, yeah, it was time to get to work.

He moved away from the window, taking his water bottle with him as he padded into the living room and sat on the sofa. His gaze went to the painting above the fireplace, the oil of a woman seated at the end of a large white tufted settee. The woman was Spanish, with dark hair and eyes, tan skin. She wore a midnight-blue dress that draped in folds. Her eyes implored you to look at her, as though she were saying the words "Look at me."

She resembled his mother so distinctly that staring at the painting always caused a hitch in his chest. Uncannily, this Mabel Alvarez original was named *Arabella in Repose*. Mom's name. Mom had been an art lover, and she'd been fascinated by Alvarez's portraits, particularly after she'd learned that the artist's favorite model had been a woman with her name.

Tonight Darius was reminded again of his father's story about the painting—a legacy, actually—and how the old guy had always attributed his good fortune of marrying the lovely Arabella Vega to his purchasing this painting. Cost him everything he had too. Now that original oil was worth a ton, according to a New York art collector who periodically touched base inquiring if he'd consider selling it. But, no. This piece of art was a piece of his heritage, his parents' story. Yeah, hearing the tale so many times annoyed him, but the history mollified him enough to keep his trap shut about it.

He pulled a thick file onto his lap and removed the elastic cinch. Lifting his laptop lid, he concentrated on the possibility of losing his job. He had no choice but to do what Parker Paper wanted and find some business that appealed more to women, some place where he could work his magic. He and the team weren't miracle workers, and the show's format was *reality*. But the ten-thousand dollars the show gave to a selected business to be used for refurbishment and marketing would certainly help somebody. The owners had to be willing to be bombarded in their day-to-day existences, tolerate a camera crew following them around like insects on a picnic blanket, capturing every move, every smile, and every tear. And the magic of the digital cutting room and the production people would turn a crazy amount of footage into one two-hour episode of *Wirth More*. All Darius had to do was find the right place.

After he did, he and Jake would need to pitch their selection to Parker Paper. This was what he needed to concentrate on at the moment, although bits and pieces of his meeting at The Memory Center knocked on the walls of his brain. He couldn't even wrap his head around what was going to happen to Pop.

He'd do some research on state-run places, check

with his financial advisor to see if he had some liquid assets he could use to pay for a little more time for his father to stay at The Center until they found a suitable new place.

For now his job was his focus. A random thought appeared in his head, though. The girl in the coffee shop, her face coming to mind again. Her petulant lip, her daring gaze. That was it. She with no money, a coat ten sizes too big, and a chin jutting up at him—she wasn't about to let her circumstance, whatever it was, swallow her. The same idea that occurred to him then came to mind now. That girl had not been wigged out about coffee. And whatever it was, he got the distinct feeling she was not going to let it get her. Tenacity. She had tenacity. And when it came to his need for a brilliant idea, so did he.

He went through some of the prospects Jake provided, turning page after page of businesses everywhere from a bakery in Concord, Massachusetts, to an ice cream shop in Bethany Beach, Delaware. There was no way in hell he could take the time to be that far away from his father's situation. No. He'd find something closer to home. He tabbed through images on his laptop, perusing establishments of downtown Sycamore River. Darius hoped to find gold.

Chapter Seven

The funeral was on Friday, and nearly the entire town of Sycamore River had shown up for Rosie Mandanello's send-off. The past few days had been a flurry of activity, talking to the man with the creepy smile at the funeral home, making arrangements with the minister at Saint Cecilia's Church.

Rylee had taken it upon herself to inform the employees of Rosie's Bridals, with Kit immediately stepping into action to help with contacting clients whose orders were pending. News travelled fast in their small town, and when word got out that Rosie had died, the frantic calls from brides-to-be came rushing in.

Kit's assistant seamstress, Freda, pitched in as well as the two sales consultants, Mary Ann and Linda. Their tutelage was testament to how much they loved Rosie. Rylee had been too busy for the truth to sink in, even when she'd stopped down at the store to check on things and post the Closed until Further Notice sign in the window. She'd been too occupied to mourn and suspected the same was true for her mother, but these days Mom wasn't easy to read with her newfound yoga-slash-meditation lifestyle.

They were back at Mom and Sonny's house now, the repast food arrayed on the dining room table. Townspeople sat in folding chairs placed here and there. The more people who came through the front door, the more fresh-baked pies were lined up on the kitchen counter.

Alone in the kitchen, Rylee stood at the island eating an apple pie right out of the tin. She was a bit of a pie snob because of her grandmother's renowned ability with fruit blanketed by dough. The woman had even owned a serious-looking apple-peeling device that looked as if it belonged on somebody's workbench.

Rylee rolled the morsel around in her mouth and assessed. She speared another bite full onto her fork and gobbled it. How odd that when someone died, everybody felt the need to eat. Eat and bake. Well, whoever had made this offering had done a bang-up job. This was one hell of a pie. The raisins were a nice touch. Rosie would have approved.

The visitors were all abuzz about Rosie, telling stories about her, laughing at anecdotes, pausing to reminisce. And the question of what would become of the shop was on everyone's lips. How word had already gotten around that Rosie had bequeathed her store to Rylee was no surprise. That's how Sycamore River worked. One person got hold of a juicy nugget, and it was all over. She couldn't wrap her brain around the idea of running the shop, not right now anyway. Because right now all she was capable of was eating pie, the button on her black skirt be damned.

The refuge in the kitchen was a tactical move to avoid the raised eyebrows and side-glances everybody seemed to be throwing her way. This was her grandmother's fault, obviously, for her outlandish request, God rest her soul. What the hell had Rosie been thinking? Was she up there in heaven playing a chess game with the Big Guy, moving the pieces of Rylee's life around? Rylee was about as prepared to run Rosie's Bridals as she was to live the rest of her life without the old woman. Even she knew there was no game once the queen was gone.

Despite her efforts to keep the images from her head, she tried to imagine Rosie as the massive stroke hit her, how she tumbled down the staircase from her apartment and snapped her hip at the socket, like an old twig. It hadn't mattered that the woman had been eighty-five. Rosie was supposed to be invincible.

Rylee pushed the swinging door that led to the dining room to see if the crowd was thinning. Around the perimeter of the room, neighbors jibber-jabbed in low voices while they balanced paper plates and disposable coffee cups in their hands. Scoffers, all of them, especially that lady who owned Snowball, the lost-then-found poodle, yet it was pretty nice of her to come, considering. She could almost tell by the looks on everyone's faces, their lipless smiles, that they had the same thought careening around in her own head—
Rosie's Bridals is doomed.

She caught sight of her mother pouring a bit of sambuca into her paper cup. In her long skirt and lace-up boots, her hand-crocheted sweater worn over a black turtleneck, the waist-long hair pulled back in a clip, she looked like a cross between a librarian and someone born in the wagon of a traveling show. But that was Angie, or rather this version of Angie. Oh-so Zen.

Mom's countenance was complacent with a kind of peaceful knowing, as if she had some kind of inside scoop that heaven was a cool place in which to take up residence. This Zen Angie morphed about a decade ago around the same time she met and then married her current husband, Sonny, an art teacher, potter, and avid gardener. The man could grow a mean batch of peppers. Sonny was the reason for her mother's calmer, more even persona. Rylee liked Zen Angie, although it was a bit disconcerting to see her mother still cool and unruffled at a time like this. But maybe that sambuca in her coffee was a contributor.

Other cordial bottles lined up on the sideboard like a makeshift bar along with petit glasses in varying shapes that Mom was proud to tell came from a rummage sale. Sonny manned the station, offering shots of deep brown, caramel-colored, and clear libations. He greeted each taker with an endearing smile and a "here you go," as he handed them a drink.

Sonny was her favorite stepfather of the three she'd had. Rylee liked him, loved him kind of, and at ten years in, this stepfather seemed to be hanging on for the long haul. She assessed the tall lanky man, a throwback to the Woodstock era with his shoulder-length hair, brown streaked with gray, and the black combat boots on his big feet in direct contrast to the pinstripe suit he wore. When Sonny retired from academia, he moved on to spending his days throwing pots on the potter's wheel he kept in the shed out in their backyard, which was now called "the studio." Clay pots and plates crammed every corner of the house. But who was Rylee to complain? It was their house, after all.

Rylee's eyes found her friend Kit, who accepted a small, stemmed glass filled with rich brown liquid from Sonny. Rylee's heart warmed. Kit was such a good egg, a trooper. Sometimes she found it hard to believe that she and Kit were the same age. Kit was so together.

Kit lifted her gaze to meet Rylee's and raised her

glass. She made her way around the maze of dining room grazers and came into the kitchen. "Are you hiding in here?"

"Want some pie?" Rylee resumed her place at the island, picked up her fork, and speared a large piece. "Apple. Really good. It's got raisins." She poked the fork in Kit's direction. "Want a taste?"

Kit put her glass on the counter and slid onto a stool. "Are we going to talk about the guts of an apple pie, my friend, or should we discuss the real topic at hand?"

Rylee put down the fork and pushed the pie tin away. "Okay. But I think I need a drink." She went to the fridge and pulled out a beer. She twisted off the top and took a long cold satisfying pull. She swallowed and locked her gaze on Kit. "You think maybe my grandmother had a loss of oxygen in her brain or something when she made the decision to put me in charge of the shop?"

Kit shook her head. "You'd really opt to believe that Rosie was demented rather than think she had faith in your ability to run the place?"

"You know me. Let's be honest. Come on. Don't you think it would behoove my grandmother's memory to have the store stay closed, become a memory, a good one, just like Rosie herself?"

"It doesn't matter what I think. Rosie believed you could do it. That says something."

Rylee took another swig of her beer. "You should run for office."

"It's not rhetoric, pal. Rosie Mandanello didn't want her legacy in this town to come to an end. The baton is yours to grab."

"I got fired as a dog walker." She shook her head. "And I nearly caused a scene in Jo-Jo's because I didn't bother to bring any cash with me when I ordered the most expensive coffee in the house. Not one of my finer moments. You should have seen me. I looked like a bag lady in that big-ass coat, and the little turd of a barista acted like I'd robbed a bank. I'm surprised nobody called the men in the white coats. I shouldn't be left to my own devices. I'm dangerous."

Kit let out a whoosh of air. "Look. About that damn dog-walking gig. The dog wasn't harmed, and you were meant for better things. And who cares about the coffee guy. I just wish you'd admit you know a lot about the bridal business. More than you think." Kit took a sip of her cordial. "You just need to believe."

Angie swooped into the room carrying one of Sonny's fired dishes that she'd used to display the brownies delivered by one of the guests. The dish was empty now. Mourners were a hungry lot.

"What are you two doing holed up in here?" She went to the sink with the dish and turned on the water. She blew air out the side of her mouth, forcing an errant lock of hair to flip away from her face. "Everybody's starting to leave." She lowered her voice, her eyelids closing half-staff. "They mean well, but I can't wait for them to go. I just want to kick off my shoes and put my feet up."

"Can I help in any way?" Kit offered.

"You can take some food with you when you leave. My God, there's a ton of it." Angie turned to Rylee. "You doing okay, honey bun?"

Rylee knew what that simple question inferred. There was no sense, however, in ticking off the ways these last few days had changed everything. "Doing okay. How about you?"

Angie came over to the island and reached to tuck back a tendril of Rylee's hair. She paused to let her fingers rest on Rylee's head. Zen Angie had a tenderness about her. "I'll tell you, though." She shook her head. "If I had a dollar for every person who asked me about you taking over Rosie's Bridals, I'd be rich." She cast her gaze to the half-eaten pie, plucked a piece of gooey apple, and popped it into her mouth. "Huh," she said. "Raisins in this one. Delish." She licked her fingers. "My mother wasn't the only one who could make a good pie." She blew out a breath, and that errant lock of hair did a dance in the whoosh. "I didn't get the pie gene."

Nor had Rylee. Her only knack was trouble. "I still haven't wrapped my brain around the fact that Rosie did this."

"You mean die? We all die, honey bun. It was her time."

"I know." A pang of guilt socked her one. Was she on the verge of making the death of her favorite person on earth all about herself? "I was talking about Rosie's Bridals, though."

"Yea." Angie tilted her head. "That's something, all right."

Kit cleared her throat. "Just want to throw this in, ladies. Rosie left Rylee the sole proprietorship of her bridal shop, one that she loved like a living, breathing relative. This wasn't some joke, and we all know she was sharp as a tack up until her last breath."

"Maybe Kit's right, honey bun." Angie shrugged one shoulder. "Rosie wanted you to have the shop for a reason. Meditate on that."

"Why didn't she just leave it to you, Mom? You're her daughter."

"Me? God, no. She left me the condo in New Port Richie."

"I know." She pointed a finger. "How about this? We'll switch. You take the shop, and I'll take the condo in Florida."

Angie chuckled. She wagged a finger at her daughter. "It's in an active adult community. You don't qualify."

That was true. There was nothing adult or active about Rylee. And most assuredly, she wasn't a candidate for owning and operating a business. Sure, she'd worked at the shop over the years, but Rosie, even at eighty-five, had still been at the helm, surrounded by Kit with her capable hands as seamstress and the two top-notch sales consultants. Rylee was a glorified clerk. She was still trying to master opening a box of satin purses or lacy garters without tearing them with the sharp edge of a cutter. She paid the invoices, pushed paper, acted as shipping and receiving. Hardly the qualifications for owning such a business.

"Do you seriously think I can just go in, turn on the lights, and step into business as usual without Rosie there? Boom. Just like that?"

Angie's mouth twisted to one side. "You could sell it and use the money to get a place of your own, maybe." She flipped her long hair over her shoulder. "Honey bun, you're welcome, though, to stay here as long as you like, you know, until everything settles down, of course."

After everything settles down? It struck Rylee as

odd. What did that mean? Rosie was gone, interred just hours ago. Her heart stalled at the thought that things would not settle down at all now that Rosie was dead.

"What are you going to do about the condo in New Port Richie?" Rylee couldn't fathom Angie and Sonny living in a planned community with rules to follow. "You thinking of moving there or anything?"

"Heck, no," she snorted. "That's going on the market. We've wanted to expand the studio and build a barn, maybe. Get some chickens."

"You're going to raise chickens? Like have a farm?"

"Maybe. Mostly we want to garden. You know, farm to table." She smiled with pride. "Fresh eggs every day. It's our dream."

Rylee couldn't help but allow a smile to take over her mouth. Who was she to question someone else's dream, scrutinize another's life? She needed to get one of those of her own.

Sonny stuck his head in around the door. "Come say goodbye, Ang. The last of them are leaving."

She grabbed a box of aluminum foil off the counter. "Not without doling out some of that pie."

****

Later, Rylee sat in her childhood bedroom. She could not believe she was back here. Again. The poster of New Kids on the Block affixed to the back of the closet door mocked her. Her head was stuffed with cotton with no room for a single clear or, God forbid, productive thought. She fell back onto the pillows and looked up at the hand-crocheted canopy draped over the points of the four posters of the French provincial bed. The lacy intricacies of the canopy were a marvel. A

51

new addition to the room, it was one of her mother's handiworks, crafted by Angie herself. Zen Angie was a living, breathing Laura Ingalls Wilder these days.

The white bedroom set had been a tenth birthday present from her mother and stepfather number one, Chuck. Chuck hadn't lasted nearly as long as this used furniture they'd found at a tag sale, but it was a pretty nice suite of canopy bed and two dressers, one nightstand. Sitting here under a frilly roof, she wondered what was wrong with her. And what the hell had made Rosie think she was ready to take on Rosie's Bridals?

She couldn't get the thought of it out of her head. It sucked to think that her grandmother's bridal shop could go down in history as a failure caused by Rylee herself. What a legacy. Her cell phone sounded, and she was grateful for the distraction. She slid her finger across the screen and connected the call.

"Hello, babe."

Freddie. Venom rushed hot at the sound of his voice. She didn't even know why it zipped around in her veins like that. She wasn't all that mad at him for finding love and moving on. *Have at it there, Freddie.* But emotions had been building up in her since the moment she'd heard the news about Rosie. She'd yet to cry a tear. Her sinus passages ached, her ears buzzed, her throat squeezed, but her eyes remained dry. Now, at just the sound of Freddie's ridiculous pet name—she hated pet names—she wanted to reach into the phone and slap the shit out of him. Even just thinking it made her feel better.

"Hi," she said.

"How are you?" His voice was contrite. Good.

Who cared?

Screw you and the horse you rode in on. She was feeling better. "Okay."

"I heard about Rosie. I'm sorry, Rylee. I know how much she meant to you."

"Yeah, um, thanks," she said, not wanting to get into a nicey-nice conversation with the guy who just dumped her on her head. She was sure now that she would have dumped him soon anyway, so there was that. "I'm getting ready to hit the sack."

"Funerals take a lot out of you, right?"

She was tired of the conversation, tired of Freddie, tired period. "Well, Freddie, thanks again for calling…"

"I'm sorry."

A stab pricked her heart. They both knew this time he was not talking about her grandmother's passing. He was talking about his decision. Well, it was her time for decision-making, and she had a whopper of one to contend with.

"Bye, Freddie."

With a swipe of her finger, she ended it.

****

She shook off the snippy edge Freddie's call invoked and began to think. The phone call had loosened that wad of cotton in her head, giving her brain some room to operate. She looked around. It was time to find a way out of this French provincial bedroom with the mocking eyes of the five members of the boy band staring back at her from the closed door. She'd drawn a heart shape with a Magic Marker around Donnie Walberg's head. She still liked him, even now, but that was beside the point. Donnie and the boys had to go.

Rylee tried to picture herself at Rosie's Bridals, living in the cute-yet-creaky little apartment upstairs, putting her own stamp on the place that right now had *Rosie* written all over its fussiness. She tried to conjure an image of herself being all businessy and successful running the store. Accolades from brides whose most important day had met all expectations thanks to her adept skills would pour like water over her life. She'd have to expand, hire more consultants, get an accountant to handle all those zeroes behind the digits of her bank account. She clicked her teeth. Was it possible that this Rylee could become that Rylee?

The bedside clock, shaped like a soccer ball, a Christmas gift from when she was fifteen, told her it was nine o'clock. The clock was from stepfather number two, Angelo. That was how she marked much of her growing up, categorizing memories by the stepfather. Angelo had been a jerk—a lying cheater, actually—but, boy, did they eat well during his reign. The man had known his way around the kitchen, and his bolognese sauce was her fondest memory of the guy.

She glanced at the clock again and bounced up off the too-soft mattress and tugged on her shoes. It didn't matter how late it was. She didn't care. The whole thing exasperated her—Rosie up and dying on her, even though she'd lived till eighty-five, the five pounds she surely had gained from eating so much damn pie, the uncertainty of everything in her life.

She had to see it tonight, feel it, maybe even experience a bit of business-type *zoom*. This was a decision that felt good to make. She was going to Rosie's Bridals.

****

"Where are you going, Rylee?" Angie loaded the dishwasher. "You missed a good dinner. We had potluck, one of those casseroles in the fridge. Chicken, cheese, broccoli. I'm going to get fat." Mom smiled as if putting on the pounds wouldn't be so bad. The old Angie, the one with Chuck who was a weight lifter, had spent much of her time in the pursuit of toned muscles. "Feel that," she had said, often thrusting her flexed arm at Rylee for her to touch the gentle bulge on her upper arm. "Nice, huh?" Fitness Angie used to say. "Pretty good, huh?"

Rylee buttoned her down jacket and tied a woolen scarf, one of Mom's handicrafts, around her neck. "I'm taking a walk."

"It's nine at night in the middle of January. It's in the teens out there and dark as all get out with no moon. Where are you going at this hour?"

"I just need some air." She didn't want to tell her mother her thoughts. Ideas about Rosie's Bridals caused a circuit overload in her brain. Instead of brain cells, she had a jumble of Christmas tree lights in her head, the strings all tangled up in each other, the tiny bulbs blinking on and off, good ideas, bad ideas, all winking in succession. But she had to go to the shop, and she had to go tonight. Nobody on this planet, herself included, thought she had it in her to run the place. Rosie's spirit was there—it had to be—and she'd commune with it, breathe it in, and if she were lucky enough, find some faith.

Angie dried a plate Sonny had made with his own hands, a fired-ceramic piece in cobalt blue. Her efforts looked like a caress. Mom was like that, now anyway.

Back years ago, she had been so consumed with finding Mr. Right after Rylee's birth father left with the announcement that he had discovered he was gay, that she'd lost herself, let alone the role of mom to the daughter that needed her. Rylee had long accepted that her childhood hadn't been anything close to the Brady Bunch. And thank God for Rosie. She'd been the mother Rylee needed when Mom was out shopping for a heterosexual mate. And Rylee was never fooled by Rosie's incessant pleading for her to come give a helping hand at the bridal salon. Rosie could run that place by herself. With her sales associates and with Kit and her helper, Freda, they had it down.

But Rylee had been so often out of work after she'd quit college she'd pretended along with Rosie that she was needed at the salon. And what started out as Rylee's answering the phone and unpacking boxes of gloves and tiaras that arrived via UPS turned into Rylee filling in with a sale, and what did she know about fashion or holding the hand of a bride whose nerves were overwrought? But maybe she could be different. The only way she'd know was to go there and see how she felt. Tonight Rylee's own nerves were as twisted as a new bride who wasn't so sure she deserved the groom.

"You're bringing a notebook with you on your walk?" Angie looked up from her delicate drying of another hand-forged dish. "You're going to walk and write?"

"I might get inspired or something. Just want to be prepared."

****

Rylee breathed in the cold night air, its bite

stinging her lungs. She expelled a cloud of vapor. Maybe opting to walk to Rosie's Bridals rather than take her car wasn't such a good idea. Her feet crunched along the frozen sidewalk, the icy patches glinting under the streetlamps along the walkway. When she got to Rosie's shop, she would sit herself down on the gold-leaf-framed settee Rosie had been so proud of—a find from a thrift shop and reupholstered in a surplus of brocade by Rosie herself—take out the notebook full of blank pages, and come up with a list. Pros and cons. Keep or sell. Stay or go.

She arrived at the storefront and just stood there for a moment and stared at the door, painted a robin's-egg blue to match the shutters on either side of the display window. Rosie's Bridals looked lost tonight. Lost and sad.

She reached into her back pocket and withdrew the key that dangled from a little chain with a pink rubber pom-pom attached to it. She placed it in her open palm. "Oh, Rosie," she said into the night. She pressed her hand to her chest. "Why in God's name did you leave this store to me? I can't even buy my own coffee."

After a moment, she inserted the key into the lock and turned. She flipped on the light switch, and the interior of the store came into view under golden light. It was quiet, still, almost like a painting she was looking at rather than a room she was standing in. Where to begin? Where to direct her attention first?

Her gaze fell to the gilded birdcage on the front desk. In it Rosie had kept a stack of her business cards. Rylee undid the little latch and opened the door. She reached in and grabbed one of the cards. She ran her thumb pad over the text, detecting a hint of rise in the lettering. She tucked the card into her notebook.

On the back of the chair was Rosie's favorite cardigan with the patch pockets. It gave off the clean, fresh scent of lavender mixed with the woodsy, earthy tinge of camphor, the oil Rosie had used on her elbows for patches of dry skin. Together the two smells were Rosie, and tonight Rylee held the garment to her face and breathed deeply.

She shed her jacket and shrugged into the oversized sweater. Feeling its comfort, she pulled it around her body like a hug. Her gaze fell to the bundle of papers on the desktop, a stack of completed contracts to be filed, a job that was typically one of Rylee's tasks, and suddenly she remembered the circumstances of the contract on top. The bride, Gracie, a nice girl, quiet, kind of timid, a little mousy, if the truth were told, had called to say she'd needed to move up her wedding because of her father's terrifying cancer diagnosis. Time was running short for Gracie to have her dad there to walk her down the aisle. So she'd come into Rosie's Bridals and found a sample that fit her like a glove, and she asked, pleaded really, if she could purchase the sample instead of waiting to order her own dress.

Rosie had a rule about that kind of thing. She didn't want to sell off her samples because replacements were a pain in the butt to get their hands on and took weeks to arrive, which put a limit on selections. She just didn't go for it. So Rylee had left her a long note about Gracie's plight and affixed it to the dress contract. Can she buy the sample? the note asked. Can we help this bride's dream wedding come true? Can we bend the rules just this once?

On top of Rylee's message, Rosie had attached one

of her signature sticky notes, a pale pink square of paper bordered by deeper-toned rosebuds. On it Rosie had written the words "Yes! Yes to it all!" She'd put a smiley face at the bottom of the note.

Rylee lifted off the note and studied the square of paper. This could have been Rosie's last act as proprietor of the store she loved so much. She slipped the paper into one of the sweater's deep pockets.

She scanned the room. Everything appeared as if suspended in time. She could almost hear the click-clack of Rosie's one-inch heels as she walked across the wooden floor, or the infectious ring of her laughter. Her presence was as big as life.

She went to a row of wedding dresses, each enclosed in a clear plastic zipper bag. Since it was January now, the dresses on the rack were for summer brides. It typically took that many months for a bride to choose a dress, order it, have it tailored, fitted, all that rigmarole. So samples were brought in months in advance of the season they were meant for. Soon enough she would have to start thinking of ordering the fall line. Rylee's heart did a little flip-flop. The thought daunted her. She'd never done the ordering, not alone anyway.

With the heat turned so low, she was still chilled despite the heavy sweater. She wished she had a hot cup of coffee, a caramel macchiato. The pirate from Jo-Jo's in his brown leather jacket came to mind, his disconcerting onyx stare. She fished his business card out from the side pocket of her purse. Darius Wirth. In the upper-left corner of the card was a logo for Living Loud TV. *Huh.* She wondered what he did for a TV station. She didn't watch much TV, especially while she'd been dating Freddie and going to all his guitar gigs at night. Now that he was gone, on his way to fame and fortune in LA, maybe she and her television would become friends. She opened her notebook, tugged the cap off her pen with her teeth, and began her to-do list with its first entry. *Pay the pirate.*

Before she could think of a next item for her list, there was rapping at the front window.

Chapter Eight

By one a.m. Darius was cross eyed. He'd gone through the file of prospective businesses, and out of maybe twenty candidates, none of them fit his need to stay close to home. His father was on borrowed time at The Memory Center, and if Darius was filming the finale up in Schenectady at a maternity shop that needed *Wirth More's* assistance or if he was down in Cape May helping build up a mother-daughter peanut-butter maker, God only knew where Pop would end up without his hand in the matter.

He went into the kitchen and popped another coffee pod into the machine. The fragrant brew with its satisfying gurgle streamed into his cup. He thought of the girl in the coffee shop, the one who'd given him such a hard time. He wondered about people. That was just something he'd done all his life. He'd see people on the beach or in line at the food store and assess their existences, pose scenarios. The girl in the shop was a perfect case to ponder with her pissy attitude contradicting the sudden cloud of sadness that came into her green-green eyes.

He lifted the cup off its stand and brought it to his lips. The coffee was too hot, and he blew over the surface. If he was going to spend any more time on the internet tonight, he needed the caffeine at his fingertips.

Back in the living room, he took a minute to just

drink the coffee and indulge in a Devil Dog he'd fished out of the freezer. He liked it when the filling was solid and the cake was cold. With a half-hearted eye, he perused the paper he'd grabbed earlier in the day. Until he'd come up to the article about Pharma-Sentra, a megadrug company, transferred to town from Texas. He sat up straighter and splayed the open paper onto the coffee table. The move had negatively affected the old timers in downtown Sycamore River, the story went on to say. The mom-and-pop shops around the green were taking a beating with newer, shinier storefronts popping up on the landscape. Where there used to be the eclectic array of businesses, there was a steady, more like relentless, gentrification. Banks, condo buildings, and trendy upscale offerings like Jabberwocky's, the place on the green with the best burgers. Darius snorted. He'd had his head up his own ass. All this time looking for the ideal business for his show's finale, and here it was in his own hometown.

He went onto the internet and did some digging. Sycamore River was suffering growing pains, for sure. Many of the townies didn't want the change thrust at them like a fist in their faces. Based on stuff he'd read in the articles from the *Ledger* and the *Record*, folks had been kicking and screaming at the new trend of their beloved town. Townies, it seemed, were a staunch brood. They wanted their eclectic downtown to remain the same.

They had had one bank on the green and that had been enough, thank you very much. But now three banks stood where charming old brick buildings had once been. The idea, Darius knew from complaints on the op-ed pages of all the local rags, was to turn the mid-Morris County town into a kind of Hoboken, very upscale with hordes of urban professionals with thick wallets descending upon the place, all too eager to spend their loot. Progress was inevitable, but somehow pushing out all the little stores pissed him off. Maybe it was because his father loved the place, his mother had loved her involvement in the town, and even though he'd moved on right after college, Sycamore River was where his roots grew. He'd all but forgotten, but now in the predawn hour, his eyes bleary from staring at the computer screen all damn night, he was sure he had to help one of the places in his hometown.

He consulted his list of town shops that appeared to be weathering the storm but not thriving as they'd been. Interestingly, Jo-Jo's Java House, the very place where he'd had the encounter with the spitfire of a woman, could be in trouble if that national coffee chain was really coming to town. The news article said it was a matter of debate at the town board meetings. Jo-Jo's wasn't really a prospect, though, because it was run by two brothers and Parker Paper wanted female influence.

Henson's was a nickel-and-dime sort of store run by mother, father, and son and had been there forever. The married couple was kind of a comical duo with their harmless bickering, and the son, Ean, had been Darius's schoolmate. There were no dollar stores in the downtown area of Sycamore River, so Henson's was hanging on, especially with Ean on board to grow business. Darius needed to find out just how much Mrs. Henson was still involved in the business. If she was there all the time, maybe he could spin it as a *female friendly* store to appease the show's main sponsor.

Then he came upon an article about a bridal salon

on the corner of Hampshire Boulevard and Main, a stand-alone brick structure, small and quaint, two stories. Rosie's Bridals. The story was an interesting one, for sure. The owner had just died. One Rose Elena Mandanello had opened the store in the sixties, and she'd served the wedding preparatory needs of generations of women in the town. Everyone, according to the local news hub, had loved the woman. The store was closed now, and if it stayed that way, he was shit out of luck. But he'd check it out, see for himself. He had a hunch about it. He was good at hunches. Tomorrow, after meeting with Parker Paper where he'd spin the save-my-hometown theme, work his magic, he would head to Sycamore River where he had work to do.

Chapter Nine

The rap at the front door startled her. Rylee was alone, and it was late. Vulnerability pricked at her skin. The front of the store was all windows, and she could make out the shadow of someone: someone tall and thin, wearing a dark jacket, peering in around hands cupped to his or her face.

She picked up a broom and with both hands held it in front of her. Not that she knew what she'd do with it if she needed to defend herself, but the grip of it felt good. She made her way slowly toward the door, straw ready.

Close up, she saw who it was and her insides unclenched, freeing her lungs to pull in air. She opened the heavy oak door and swung it wide. Kit peeked over the folds of a thick scarf and lifted a woolen hand to give a shy little wave.

"Kit! You scared me to death. What are you doing here?"

"Can I come in?" Kit gave an exaggerated shiver. "It's an icebox out here. And put down that broom."

Rylee let the broom go with one hand, and the straw bottom tapped to the floor. She stepped aside for Kit to enter.

"You're wearing Rosie's sweater. I smell her."

Rylee smiled. She snuggled into the sweater, tucking her head to her shoulder, and drew in the scent of her grandmother. She closed her eyes and willed the garment to never lose Rosie from its fibers. "Yeah, me too."

Kit unwound the scarf from around her neck and shrugged out of her down jacket. "So whatever you're doing couldn't wait till morning?"

"How'd you find me?"

"You didn't answer my texts, so I called the house and talked to your mom. She said you had gone for a walk and that you didn't say where. When she said you had a notebook with you, I knew you'd be here." She walked over to a wooden chair and placed her coat and paraphernalia on it. Looking around, she made her way to the desk. She flipped open the notebook with one finger and eyeballed the words Rylee had just scrawled on line one. "What's this?"

"My list. I think I need to be a list person. Rosie was a list person. That's the beginning of a list, anyway."

"Um, Rylee, pal, lists can be a great tool, but it says here 'Pay the Pirate.'" Kit laughed and lifted her gaze. "Did you mean 'Pay the Piper'?"

"Nope. The pirate's the guy who paid for my coffee at what I've come to call the 'Jo-Jo's Incident.'"

"Yeah, you never elaborated on how that went. All you said was that you nearly caused a scene, which seemed a bit extreme, but under the circumstances I figured you were just high strung from, you know, the funeral and stuff. Besides, how come the clerk at Jo-Jo's didn't just trust you to come back and pay up? You're there all the time."

"Noooo." She shook her head. "There's a new barista in town, and he wasn't about to let me get off easy."

"So this random guy offered to pay for it. How's that nearly causing a scene? It's nice." Kit flashed a grin. "Sir Galahad lives and breathes."

Rylee snorted. "Um, no. He was a pirate."

"Pirates go to Jo-Jo's? Did he park his ship out front?"

"Not a pirate pirate. He was one of those yuppies in off the train who happened to look like a pirate. All he needed was an eye patch."

Kit just stared at her.

"I'm serious."

"What's a pirate look like these days, anyway?"

Rylee leaned the broom against a wall and put her hands on her hips. She sighed. "Tall, but not real tall, black hair so black it looked blue, pissy look on his carved-granite face, cheekbones like a cliff side, his mouth a slash. You know—Black Beard. But no beard." She swept her hand toward the row of dresses on the rack. "So, anyway, I'm here to decide what to do."

"You've got quite the eye, Rylee. A police sketch artist would love someone like you."

"Well, I've got to pay him so I can tick that off my list." She clutched the notebook into her hands. "I'm going to list pro and con. Sell or..." She ran a hand through her hair. "Or what, Kit? Who am I kidding? Could I really do this?"

"My guess is that if you came here tonight with such determination that it couldn't wait until a decent time of day that you kind of know the answer is right there." Kit pointed to the center of Rylee's chest. "Right where you tick."

Rylee couldn't help but smile. This woman who had made a name for herself here at Rosie's Bridals, who could now be a much-sought-after seamstress at any high-end department store or with a New York design firm, had become a dear friend. Her eyes stung with suppressed tears. "Come with me upstairs to the apartment."

She couldn't go there alone. Her mother was the only one who had been to the apartment since Rosie's death. She'd gone to retrieve the dress Rosie had specified she'd wanted to be buried in, the ecru-toned lace sheath with the bolero jacket.

"Come on, pal. Let's go." Kit hooked her arm with Rylee's.

****

The apartment was small, and when Rylee snapped on the tableside lamp, the warm yellow light gave the smart living room a storybook hue. An image popped into her head of Rosie sipping her nightly glass of cabernet, feet up on the needlepoint step stool, head back on the tapestry of her wing chair. Her heart ached for the woman.

She turned to her friend, feeling her eyes sting again. "I miss her."

"Me too," Kit said in a low reverent tone. "I feel her here. You?"

Rylee nodded, unable to speak the word. But, yes, she felt the presence of Rosie Mandanello. It was like standing in the rain naked, no part of her unaffected. She placed a hand on the wing of the chair and gave it a squeeze, sinking her fingers into its cushion. The upset of this day, the funeral, the whispers of townsfolk at Mom's house during the repast, her own insecurity about the shop—all of it lifted, released its clasp on her insides. She could almost feel the fog of indecision burn off in the warm memories of this space.

She swallowed against the ache in her throat. Her eyes found the thick photo album Rosie had kept like a coffee-table book. The cover was a print she'd copied from an anniversary edition of *The Saturday Evening Post*. This cover appeared June 1931, the year Rosie was born, and it was a photo of a bride and groom on their wedding day. The text along the bottom of the photo indicated that inside the edition was a short story by Sinclair Lewis, "Ring Around a Rosy." This had been Rosie's absolute favorite thing in the room, this binder full of bride's stories, thank-you notes, and photographs of beaming brides in their beautiful gowns on their special days. This tome was Rylee's favorite item as well. It occurred to her now that this print on the cover was like a prophet's snapshot into what the young Rose Elena, born that year, would be when she was grown up. An owner of a bridal store that worked the magic that was a wedding.

Rylee sat on the sofa and opened the binder. Kit took a seat beside her. In silence she turned the pages, the suction of the plastic that covered the pages the only sound in the room. They slowly scanned the memorabilia of all the brides from over all the years. Rylee turned to Kit and touched fingers to her arm. "It's a lot to ask, Kit," she said thickly.

"Rosie wouldn't have asked if she didn't think you could carry on her legacy."

Rylee's lips trembled as they curved into a smile. "That's not what I meant." She took a shivery breath. "I know you could probably write your own ticket anywhere that needs a brilliant seamstress, and I know you could probably make a ton more money..."

Kit sucked in her breath and clapped a hand to her mouth. "Yes!"

"Yes?" Now Rylee did not care that the tears in her eyes were so plentiful they tumbled down her face. They were a relief. "You'll help me do this?"

The two friends embraced in the small living room that would now become Rylee's home. She was doing this. Holy mackerel. Holy freakin' mackerel.

Chapter Ten

Parker Paper was totally on board with Darius's idea of choosing a business in his hometown. Pleasing the suits with the wallets made Jake a happy producer, even though they still hadn't signed with a needy business for the last episode. But Parker Paper loved the idea of the bridal shop. Checking out Rosie's Bridals in person was on Darius's agenda, but first he was heading to Sycamore River to meet with Toni from The Memory Center to discuss options for Pop. Jake went with him to the station while he waited for his train.

"You did good, Darius." Jake cuffed him on the shoulder. "Now you've got to seal the deal."

"Since I'll be in Sycamore River for the day, I'll make the time to check out the bridal shop and see what I can learn about its future. With any luck, they'll be reopening and we can cut a deal."

"Use that *Wirth More* persuasion of yours," Jake said. "Hey, speaking of your hometown, I hear you had an altercation at a coffee shop there."

"What?" How did Jake get his news? He didn't miss a frickin' beat, ever. "What are you talking about *altercation?*"

A laugh shot from him like a cannonball. "Some college kid sent a video to our website. It was you and some kind of odd woman having an issue with her inability to pay for coffee. The kid's commentary was a riot. You should see it."

"Well, it wasn't an altercation. The woman forgot her wallet and held up the line for a while until she agreed to let me pay for her coffee."

"Seemed kind of psycho."

"I don't know how psycho she was, but, yeah, she was adamant."

The train whooshed into the station, and the two men shook hands. "Keep me posted, Darius," Jake said. "Good luck with your meeting about your father."

"Thanks, Jake."

"And stay away from crazy women in coffee shops."

Darius saluted him. Yes, he'd steer clear of that type of distraction.

****

"Well, look at you this morning," Zen Angie said as she slid scrambled eggs onto Sonny's plate from a tilted fry pan. "Want some eggs, Rylee?"

"No, thanks," she said, impressed her mother noticed she'd taken some time with herself this morning. Her shower had been long and hot, and she had taken her time blowing out her hair. She sported a decent outfit, although her jeans were a bit snug thanks to her newfound penchant for apple pie.

"You look nice," Sonny said, then slid his gaze back to the woman who'd made his breakfast. "Thanks for breakfast, babe." That was another thing about this newfangled mother of hers. This one cooked. There was no end to Zen Angie's talents.

"I didn't have time to talk with you guys last night when I got home. It was late."

"Yes." Her mom took a seat beside Sonny at the

72

island. "By the way, Kit called last night after you'd left."

"Yeah, she found me. I was at the shop."

Zen Angie looked up from her eggs, a triangle of toast held aloft. "What on earth made you have to go to the shop at that late hour?"

"To decide on what to do." Her body stiffened, her muscles bracing against what Angie and Sonny would say. But it was now or never. "Not selling the place after all. I'm going to take over."

Two wide-eyed gazes locked on her for a long moment before the egg-eating duo shared a glance. Sonny's Adam's apple bobbed in a swallow. Angie put down her fork and placed her elbows on the countertop.

"Honey bun, you might want to take some more time to, you know, think that through. It's not easy running a business."

"I know." Her chest beat with a warning signal. *Don't listen to her,* her heart thumped. Yet the old doubt fluttered into her gut. The embedded doubt that she could actually succeed, the doubt that she could choose well. It wasn't just theory either. History had a way of slamming home that she'd given doubt every reason to take residence inside her. Zen Angie's eyes were bugged out, and she'd forgotten how to blink.

"Mom, Sonny," Rylee said. "I realize that this is taking on a lot, but I'm ready. I've worked in Rosie's Bridals for most of my life. Off and on, granted, but still. And Kit's going to stay on board as the seamstress. I'm planning to contact the sales consultants today to see if they want to work for me." Just saying "work for me" almost made her charge to the fridge for some leftover pie, but she held her ground. "Be glad for me."

73

"Of course we're glad for you." Sonny's gaze was locked on his wife as he recited his statement with a coaxing intonation, an obvious invitation for his wife to chime in with positive support.

But Zen Angie did not chime. She picked up a piece of her whole-wheat toast and bit off the end. She chewed silently, the loudest silence Rylee had ever heard.

"Let us know if we can help." Sonny slipped an arm around Angie's shoulders. "Right, honey?"

Finally, Angie met her daughter's eyes. "Baby girl, I just don't want you to set yourself up for disappointment. You've had enough of that."

Rylee stifled the urge to remind her mother that, yes, she had suffered an inordinate amount of disappointment in her life, and lots and lots of it stemmed from Angie's brand of parenting throughout the years. There was no sense in getting into that, though. What good would it do to cut her mother with sharp words? An accusation like that would linger in her head all day, sour like a pile of compost, clouding the important things she had to accomplish.

She pinned on a smile. "I'm going in eyes wide open, Mom. I feel good about it."

Angie nodded. "Okay, then. The decision is made." She chewed her toast.

****

Darius left the Sycamore River train station and strode in the direction of Maple Avenue where Jo-Jo's Java House waited with its fresh hot Brazilian blend. Jo-Jo's was his favorite. This was a good town. He feasted his eyes on the sites with nostalgia's eye, the clock tower atop the town hall building, the park in the middle of the square. It was quiet there today, the benches along the walkways empty. The air was too cold.

He pulled the collar of his coat up around his ears. Head down, he tramped along the sidewalk to Jo-Jo's. He entered and took his place in the typical line that reminded him of a gas station with a trail of cars waiting to fuel up. The door opened behind him, and a rush of cold air hit the back of his head.

Darius heard her voice and knew it was her before he even had to turn around. And there she was, the girl with the cat eyes, and she wasn't frazzled one bit this morning. She was with another young woman, but his eyes were only interested in her. She'd shed her baggy overcoat, and today she sported a short quilted jacket that stopped at her waist. He noticed the nice pair of dark jeans that fit her well, particularly in the ass. She had a nice one. Her hair was combed and shiny like a chestnut's shell, and it was pulled into a high ponytail that swished as she approached him. She wore gold hoop earrings, and her nice lips shone with an application of gloss. Her cat eyes were bright and, frankly, stunning in the daytime. So much for thinking she hadn't been much to look at. Right now he couldn't pull his gaze away.

He fixed his eyes on her. "Caramel macchiato, extra caramel," he said before he could think not to.

"Oh." Her gaze darted to her friend and back at him. "Hi."

"Good morning." He felt his mouth curve upward. Why did this woman amuse him so?

"I, uh, am glad I ran into you." She rifled through her satchel and withdrew a patchwork leather wallet. "It gives me the chance to pay you back for the coffee." She unzipped the wallet and pulled out a five-dollar bill. Handing it to him, she said, "Keep the change."

He accepted the bill because he didn't want to argue with her again. "Thank you. But like I said that night, it was no big deal."

After an awkward moment, he turned to face forward again. He heard her friend whisper, "So that's your pirate?"

"Shhhh…"

The words gave him a jolt, a reason to turn around. So he did. "What'd she just say?"

"Nothing."

"Yes, she did."

"No. Uh-uh. Nothing."

He looked at the friend. "Did you just call me a pirate?"

They were a silent pair, saucer-eyed. The girl from that night looked scared shitless, and he couldn't figure out why it cracked him up as much as it did.

"It's, um, your turn," The caramel-macchiato girl pointed toward the counter. "Wouldn't want to hold up the line now, would we?"

After placing his order with the barista, he heard her companion apologize, and the caramel macchiato girl said, "You're going to get me into trouble."

And then the giggle. Caramel Macchiato Girl had a nice giggle, and when he handed his payment for his black, no sugar, he stifled his own grin. *A pirate, huh?*

So she'd told the coffee story to her friend. He had no idea why it mattered one way or the other. Although she looked pretty damn good today—there was no denying it—he was not in the market for starting up with another woman on any level. He just didn't want the hassle. And that was where he and Jake differed as well. His boss and college roommate dated as though it were an Olympic sport.

"Enjoy your day, ladies," he offered as he passed them on the way out the door. He flashed a quick smile, and a warm flush climbed her cheeks. She met his gaze with hooded eyes and gave a little nod. That little nod jabbed her insides, which made no sense whatsoever.

****

Rylee trod beside Kit along the cold sidewalk. She did her best to quell the niggle of buyer's remorse that intermittently pinched her gut. It was one thing last night to take a stand amidst the coziness and nostalgia of her grandmother's apartment. It was another in the light of day to grasp what she'd signed up for. Her chitchat with Mom and Sonny this morning hadn't helped matters one single bit.

"So you were right about the guy," Kit said, interrupting Rylee's train of thought. "He does look like a pirate."

Rylee pulled her gaze over to her companion. "Yeah, well, at least I was able to pay him back. That's done. Can't wait to tick it off my list."

"He's a looker, though, huh?"

"As far as pirates go."

"He looks familiar, though, for some reason."

"You're thinking about the time you saw Peter Pan. The pirate was the bad guy."

When they arrived at the shop, Rylee pulled out her key, and the two of them entered. It was cold inside, the heat having been turned down, and that was where it was going to stay until she had things settled. No sense in having to pay an exorbitant energy bill.

She took off her jacket and threw it onto the settee. She pulled out her notebook and consulted the list she had begun last night. "Okay. The pirate's done. Now I need to go over the list of samples. The ones that are not embossed with the word *sample* are good for resale. So I'm going to start with those."

Kit put her hands on her hips. "Run it by me again why we're selling off all the dresses?"

"I'm going to need some cash if I'm going to get things ready to reopen. I'll need to order soon enough for the upcoming season."

Kit started at one end of the rack of dresses while Rylee began at the other. One by one they inspected the dresses, unzipping each bag and pulling the garments free. They made a pile of dresses to sell on eBay.

"You're going to need a marketing budget as well," Kit said. "Are you keeping the name of the place?"

"Of course," Rylee said. "This will always be Rosie's Bridals." She folded a dress over her arm. "Am I doing the right thing, Kit?"

"Don't second-guess it." Kit flashed a quick look and went back to studying the dresses wrapped in plastic bags. "I knew that's what's going on in your pretty little head. But, seriously, don't."

"I'm thirty years old."

"So?"

"So I've been back living with my parents because I lost my apartment due to the fact that I picked a doozy of a roommate who turned out to be a thief, and then money went out the window when I got fired for losing someone's prized poodle. Who knows how I even got through the holidays? I just hope I'm not deluding myself about this. You should have seen my mother's face this morning. It was like I told her I'm getting a sex-change operation."

"We know how your mom can be. Don't take on her hesitation."

"Well, the fact that this whole plan will get me out from under her roof is a powerful motivation. So I'll try to keep that in the front of my mind."

"That is an incentive," Kit said with a smirk.

"I don't mean to be so tough on my mom. On the Angie-o-Meter, she's off the charts these days, you know? Granted, it took a failed marriage with my father followed by two ridiculously awful new husbands until she met Sonny and found her quote, unquote calling. She was in her late forties when she technically started behaving like a responsible adult. My father, well, he was in his thirties when he realized that, oh yeah, he was a gay American. So it took him that long to even discover who he was. Are you seeing a pattern here, Kit?"

"You're fishing for reasons to keep that doubt alive and well."

"Just stating the facts."

"Those aren't *your* facts, Rylee. What your parents did doesn't mean it's your legacy. This," Kit said with her arms wide. "This is your legacy."

Rylee's heart swelled. Dear Rosie Mandanello and her unconditional faith in her only granddaughter. If it killed her, she'd honor that old gal. Her parents' issues were not hers, but God help her when she decided to pick a life partner. Rosie had tried coaching her on that front as well. Rosie knew her daughter had been no one to give tips on how to pick a guy. Rylee's mom had a bad habit of marrying first and then finding out they were Mr. Wrong.

She loved her mother. She did. But Angie had morphed into so many versions of herself over the years, and even from a tender age, Rylee had had to adapt to all those versions. There was the "got to find a man who isn't gay Angie" she'd been when Rylee's father first left. That was when Rylee was around ten years old and when she had begun to bond like glue to Rosie. She and her grandmother made the cupcakes for the bake sales. She and her grandmother had worked on book reports, dioramas, posters, and papier-mâché figurines. Rosie had taught her the way extra-cold butter made for flakier piecrust. Stuff like that.

Then when Angie met stepfather number one, she had morphed into a leather-jacket-wearing woman who suddenly liked motorcycles and tattoos. Angie had a tattoo of a leafy vine that wound around her left ankle.

The second stepfather brought a different Angie. She'd gone by *Angela* in those days, and their house smelled of oregano and basil most of the time with his Italian cooking. But he'd turned out to be a lying jerk who enjoyed the effects of illegal substances, and even Angie had a limit.

After the second remarriage, Mom had taken a break from men and worked on getting her own act together. It was a good time for Rylee. Angie did her best to be the mom she thought Rylee needed. Rylee had been sixteen then, and now she was the first to admit she had been less than lovely to be around. Her favorite pastime had been watching old movies on television and eating Cheez Doodles right out of the bag. It was a chubby time for Rylee, and the girth made her cranky. What a cruel twist of fate that she'd finally gotten an attentive mother when she just wanted to be left the hell alone.

Eugene Dalton, who went by *Sonny*, came along around the time Rylee was about to graduate high school. Her mother dating an art teacher in Rylee's school had been awkward. Word spread fast because that was what Sycamore River did with gusto—gossip. Rylee had been prepared to hate him just because that seemed like the thing to do with Angie's men, but try as she had, she just couldn't dislike Sonny. He was affable enough, helped around the house, and he made her mother laugh with her head thrown back and her mouth open.

Angie blossomed into a cool and calm person who hummed to herself all the time, learned about yarn and needle sizes, took up crochet. She found yoga and meditation. Sonny bought her a loom. She became a very likeable Angie. *Namaste.*

Rylee's father, well, what was there to say about a man who married, had a daughter, and then decided one day that he didn't want to be a car salesman anymore but wanted to be an actor, and, oh yeah, he was gay? So Dad was alive and well these days living in San Francisco with someone named Dean, and they were both pursuing their passion for acting while working as line chefs in a waterfront restaurant.

The only one in her lineage who knew how to choose a mate and choose a life was Rosie. She and Grandpa Sal had been something. Although he died when Rylee was just a teenager, she knew the love those two shared. The handholding, the shared giggles, the playful razzing of each other. The way Grandpa would show up at the salon with Rosie's favorite sandwich from the deli and say "Thought you could use salami and provolone on a kaiser roll."

It was their brand of love. A simple sandwich that said it all. *I know you love this, and I love you, so here I got it for you.* She hadn't had to wonder if Rosie and Sal experienced that elusive *zoom* when they were within a few feet of each other. Even with gray hair and the smell of Ben Gay, those two still felt it.

Rylee envied that fairy-tale kind of love, but she feared in her heart that it was reserved for Rosie and Sal and people from their generation. Not for a thirty-year-old who agonized on how to tell her boyfriend she hadn't wanted to move in with him, all while he was falling in love with Abigail, the magically delicious triangle player.

"What are you thinking?" Kit asked. "I see your wheels going on in your head."

"I'm just thinking about Freddie and how wrong I was about him."

"Oh, so what? You weren't that into him anyway. No, as you say, *zoom*. Am I right?"

An image of Darius Wirth and the coffee-buying incident popped into her mind. The pirate with the dark skin and the flashy eyes and, goddamn it all, the man whose proximity had made her blood flow quicken and caused her heart to jolt up, then down. And wasn't it just her luck that meeting the guy had been screwy and he'd overheard the pirate comment to boot? If he ever saw her again, he'd probably run the other way. Nice.

"You're not the only one that's dabbled in dead-end relationships," Kit said. "Don't forget my lovely situation with Mike."

"Stupid Mike," Rylee said. Mike had been Kit's college boyfriend. They'd moved in together and had been on the path to happily ever after when he decided it wasn't working. So he moved out, quit his job, and who knew where he was these days. Men.

"Yeah, no more stupid men."

"Definitely."

"Does that include pirates?"

Rylee threw a wad of paper at her.

****

After going to The Wedgewood Home for the Aged in Madison, Darius felt like crap. His father was not going there. He didn't care how he'd finagle it, but no, even though the home was the most affordable option before hitting the list of state-run facilities The Memory Center had provided him. He had hoped that The Wedgewood would have turned out to be the answer. But with its water-stained ceiling tiles, smell of puke or something in the air that made you want to puke yourself, and dour-faced staff members who didn't even look you in the eye, no way.

It was lunchtime, and he found himself again in Jabberwocky's. But instead of one of those signature burgers, he ordered himself a grilled chicken salad. And a beer. The Wedgewood's sad-looking façade with droopy shutters about to fall from their wrought-iron hinges and the heavy satin drapes in the office that looked like a goddamn funeral home called for a pint of ale.

He'd purchased a copy of a daily newspaper that included the part of Morris County in which Sycamore River was located. He hoped for more insight for the show.

The cover story was all about the highway improvements on the fringes of Morristown, the county seat, and how traffic would be a pain in the ass for a while. The bridge on Bethany Lane was part of the improvements, and the anticipated completion wasn't until sometime in the summer. Morristown's traffic pattern would surely impact Sycamore River, considering the town was just south of it by way of Route 202. That could be good news for Sycamore River if commuters used their downtown while construction put a snag in Morristown traffic. Feeling a glimmer of anticipation, Darius read on, turning to page 5A where the story continued.

And there it was at the top of page 5A, just below an ad for the Elk's Club's annual pancake breakfast, blaring at him like a beacon on a foggy shoreline.

The photograph of the old lady from the bridal shop who'd recently passed away, the owner of the place that was top on his list for *Wirth More*. Rosie Mandanello, with her gray hair puffed up and sprayed stiff, looked into the lens of someone's camera with crinkly-cornered lively eyes, as if she had a secret she wasn't about to share. She was standing inside her store, Rosie's Bridals on Main Street. Why hadn't he ever laid eyes on the place? Granted, the storefront was small and tucked in between the Ladies Club and a mom-and-pop pharmacy. More to the point, though, was that he shied away from all things wedding. He was reminded of Caroline's ultimatum. His former girlfriend had wanted marriage and babies. Darius wasn't that guy. He'd wanted to kick himself for anything he'd done or said that made Caroline believe forever was where they'd been headed. There was no altar in his future then or now or ever. It wasn't that he didn't believe in love and all that. He did. But at thirty-five, he'd never once felt as if he'd better sell his boat, not that he had a boat, to buy a painting so a woman would agree to be his bride.

His parents' story was unique, granted, and that kind of all-in love didn't happen to people on a regular basis. And that was fine. Darius's life was easier that way. Less mess. That kind of love had its price. Pop's intense mourning had to have played a part in his mind's fogginess, even acting like a big fat eraser to his mind. Who'd sign up for that?

As he munched his salad, he read the entire human-interest piece. He'd already known the stuff about the bridal shop, that it had closed with Rosie's death, but the article went on to elaborate on Sycamore River's struggle to keep their old-town feel. With all the new restaurants and megabanks, little shops like Rosie's Bridals were becoming a thing of the past. The scenario was ideal for *Wirth More*. He had to find out the scoop on the place.

Chapter Eleven

Up in the apartment Rylee and Kit worked through the morning, past lunch, and into the afternoon. Finally, they took a break and assessed their progress.

With all the superfluous stuff boxed, bagged, or put out for the garbage pickup and all the necessary things put in proper places, Rylee could actually see some decent progress in the space that she just might start to call home.

"I can't believe it," she said. "Thanks for helping with all this."

"We did good," Kit said.

Kit and her smile had a way of making Rylee believe that maybe she wasn't such a screwup after all. When Kit first crossed the threshold to Rosie's Bridals as the new seamstress, she'd appeared so young, but, man, had she impressed Rosie with her tailoring skill. Rylee remembered feeling a tinge of jealousy. She'd wished she had some true skill. But her jealousy hadn't lasted long because she and Kit had bonded in record time, and on some gut level Rylee knew she could trust her. She didn't get that feeling often. With all her bad choices in life, particularly in boyfriends along the way, she needed to be more discerning when it came to forging a bond of any kind. She'd been easily fooled. No more.

"What do you say we reward ourselves with a

turkey club at Jabberwocky's?"

Kit waved her hands in the air. "Hell, yeah."

****

Rylee looked at her friend across the table. How had all this happened to her in a matter of days? Despite the whirlwind of activity, she was enjoying a glimmer of lightheartedness for the first time since Rosie's death. She didn't know how she was going to pull this off, but for today, with this big sandwich that was just awesome, she was happy.

Then her gaze, as she casually scanned the midday crowd at Jabberwocky's, landed on the pirate. Something stirred inside her, a kind of spark. And she knew without a doubt she had learned nothing whatsoever about men. Because that little niggle low in her belly right now was bad, very bad. That champagne she'd just indulged in because Kit had insisted they order it over a diet Coke apparently had control of her eyeballs, which were now happily fixated on Darius Wirth and that shock of black hair that fell over his forehead à la Superman. God help her.

"That's him again," Kit said sotto voce.

"Don't look, though."

"Why not? You are."

He was at the bar. His legs, taut looking and strong in his indigo jeans, straddled the stool.

"That's one delicious-looking son of a bitch."

"I'd pretend I hadn't noticed, but I have eyes that work." They both shared a chuckle. "But he's probably married, and he thinks I'm insane, I'm sure, and I suck at men, so, yeah, I'm pretending he's an inferno and if I go near him, I'll spontaneously combust."

Now Kit laughed, a good hearty sound that made

87

Rylee laugh as well. She instantly felt the lightness again, the luckiness of having a purpose, having a place of her own that didn't include Zen Angie, and having Kit as her friend. Her gaze flitted over to the pirate again. The way he straddled that seat made her wish she had been born a stool. She never had those thoughts about Freddie, not even when she first saw him that night at the coffeehouse where he was playing acoustic guitar and singing pleasant renditions of folk songs. Freddie never made her wish she'd been born a stool so he could straddle her.

Rylee pushed her plate away, leaving the french fries that came with the sandwich untouched. She had to stop eating so much. Rosie's funeral food had done her in. That and her nerves. Her nerves craved carbs and sugar and fat. Hence, the pie overload and the bag of peanuts M&M's that somehow had found its way into her shopping basket when she'd gone to the food store for basic supplies.

She looked up to see Mr. Darius Wirth headed to their booth. He had a slanty smile on his face, his black eyes meeting her gaze. The tinge of heat flickering in her veins unnerved her. A warm sensation climbed up her face. Yes. He was a bonfire, and she must not get too close.

"Hi again, ladies," he said.

"Hi," they said in unison and shared a look. God, this hunk of man needed to get out of her line of vision soon. An urge to bite something taunted her. She plucked a fry from her dish and bit off the end with her front teeth.

"Enjoy the rest of your day," he said with that slanty mouth of his.

After he strode by, leaving a waft of pine forest scent in his wake, Rylee pulled her gaze over to Kit, who stared back with round eyes. "What?"

"You should see what you look like right now, pal."

Rylee reached up to touch her own cheek, which was hot from the flame of him.

"I've never seen you react to a guy like that."

Now that he was gone, she swallowed hard and breathed in the leftover spiciness in the air. Yeah, that guy had to stay gone.

****

Rylee sat at the counter in her parents' kitchen, her head scrambled with ideas of what she had to do. Packing up her stuff, moving, tackling getting the shop ready for reopening.

The stack of unpaid bills was a disconcerting find, considering Rosie had never once seemed worried about any debt. If it weren't so daunting, it would be funny, a riot even, to think she'd been put in charge of the debits and credits of business. Putting up some of the sample dresses on eBay would bring in some money, but not nearly enough to cover everything. Uncertainty waved at her from a proximity, a mocker just waiting for her to fall face down. She breathed deep and squared her shoulders. *Bite me, doubt.*

So much had changed in a few days. She couldn't explain it, but despite the sorrow of losing Rosie and being thrust into capitalism with the readiness of a kindergartener being placed in AP Trig, she hadn't felt so right in a long time, if ever. But for the moment, her mother burst into the room carrying a basket filled with laundry. Rylee knew from experience what that meant, and it had nothing whatsoever to do with freshly dried clothing that needed folding. This was not about matching socks. Angie wanted to talk.

"Help me fold." Angie plopped the basket onto the island's surface.

The back door burst open, and Sonny came clamoring in, his arms laden with books thick as bricks, volumes on pottery. He'd been throwing clay back in his workshop, the telltale gray specs of the stuff on his face, in his hair, and over his black sweatshirt. He smiled when he saw them. "Hi, you two."

Angie's mouth curved into an easy smile, and she all but batted her eyes at the man. Sonny wasn't exactly a heartthrob of a guy with the bald spot on the crown of his head and the unruly tuft of brown hair in front of it, the straggly ponytail that trailed down his back. Overly long scrawny neck, crazy-huge Adam's apple, but he might as well have been George Clooney the way Angie behaved around him. Rylee folded a pair of his white tube socks into a ball and silently thanked God for Sonny.

"You two look like you're in cahoots about something." He reached into the fridge and withdrew a bottle of water. "Anybody care for one?"

"Sure," Angie said. "Rylee?"

"No, thanks." She let out a breath. A question hung in the air above them, like clothes on a line drying in the breeze.

"Sonny, come here, babe," Angie said. "I was just about to ask Rylee about her plans for the store."

"Ah." He came up to the counter.

Angie twisted off the cap of her water and took a swig. Her gaze flitted over to Rylee, oh so nonchalant.

"I think you should reconsider, not to stomp all over your hopes or anything, but I just think you might be getting in over your head. You know how you are, honey bun."

Now this was like the good old days before Angie discovered meditation and yoga. Her jaw was set, her mouth pulled into a seam. Ire bubbled in Rylee's veins, hot as a pot of water on a high flame. The familiar fire was the reminder of how she'd spent many times in her life trying to figure out why Angie had always seemed to be standing there ready with an extinguisher.

"Mom," she said in an anchoring kind of way, the tone for both her mother and herself. "I'm confused here. Haven't you guys told me time and again whenever I'd get down about another dead end, that when the right thing came along I'd know it? Well, this is it. I know it. I can't figure out why you're giving me a hard time."

"I'm trying to protect you, Rylee. I'm your mother. That's what mothers do." She yanked her water bottle from the counter and swigged long. She swallowed, and with her neck craned upward, she uttered to the ceiling on an exasperated breath. "Why can't she see that?"

Rylee shook her head. Once again, this conversation had pivoted to Angie and her feelings. Her mother needed a yoga session, stat.

"Rylee, who besides me is going to be honest enough with you about this? What happens when you decide you're in over your head?" Angie waved a pair of tighty-whities at her. "Or when you decide you don't feel like being a bridal store owner anymore and would rather go scuba diving or rock climbing or something. I'm being realistic because somebody has to be."

She hadn't let her mother hurt her like this in years. She'd done such a good job in guarding herself from the lack of support. But she'd had her grandmother through all that time, and it had been Rosie who'd worked to lift her from Angie's barbs. Without Rosie at her side, the awfulness that had been their mother-daughter relationship over the years came flooding back like a torrent of angry rain. Zen had not shown up in this morning's Angie. And all Rylee could do was look over to Sonny and will him to do something quick to bring Zen Angie back.

He held her gaze for a long moment, his mouth pulled into a thoughtful bunch. He let out a long breath, scratched his bald spot. "Ang, honey…"

With that, Angie began to cry. She pulled a clean white T-shirt out of the laundry basket and held it up to her face. Her sobs were loud and deep, and they scared the hell out of Rylee. Sonny went to his wife and wrapped her in his big safe arms. She continued to cry against his shoulder, the T-shirt wedged between her face and his shirt. She mumbled words, and damned if Rylee could decipher what she was saying, but Sonny did understand because he was nodding and saying "I know, baby. I know."

"Look." Rylee swallowed her dejection like a whole bagel she'd forgotten to chew. "I need to go."

Angie lifted her head from Sonny's shoulder and stepped away from him. She wiped her face with the now-wrinkled, soggy T-shirt. "Wait."

Rylee did as she was told. She waited. The clock on the white enamel vintage stove clicked like a bomb, and her own heart thumped in time.

"Honey bun," Angie said. Sniffing loudly, she

squeezed her eyes closed. She held up a hand that said "give-me-a-minute." She breathed in deeply and blew air out of pursed lips. "Wow. I don't even know where that came from."

If Angie was looking for Rylee to give her a bye on this, she was out of luck. It was no longer her job to help Angie over one of her outbursts, even if it had been years since Rylee had seen one. Now *she* was mad.

"Maybe I should let you two talk." Sonny stepped toward the doorway to the hall.

"No," Rylee said. "It's fine, Sonny. I'm leaving."

"Honey bun, please wait." Desperation coated Angie's words, thick and drippy like too much paint on a brush. "There's something I want to say."

But Rylee turned to go.

"You can't leave like this," Zen-Free Angie moaned.

This was not new. Angie was good at slinging guilt, but mostly she was stellar at being the wounded. It was tiring, but after all, this was her mother's house, so she kept her trap shut. She met Angie's eyes and saw the repentance in them. That was the good old Angie. Outburst, then apology. She was instantly sad. Sad that not even the love of the good Sonny Dalton nor the habit of sitting cross-legged in front of a burning candle while chanting "om" could permanently erase Angie's dysfunction. Rylee's heart softened.

"Mom, look, I'm not moving to Europe. I'll just be downtown. We'll have plenty of time to talk. Okay?"

"Maybe all three of us should talk." Angie's words were watery. "We're a family the three of us."

"Yes, of course."

That was another thing. Even though Sonny had been her stepfather for almost eleven years, an all-time record as far as stepfathers were concerned around here, Mom always sought justification for his existence in their lives. She had done that with the others, but now that Sonny was permanent—dear God, he had to be— Angie was still doing it. It didn't make sense, but that was Mom. The woman knew the brand of hell she'd put her daughter through while she was growing up, parading new father candidates in like new sofas, but that was behind them. Her mother was about to turn sixty. Who needed to dredge that stuff up anymore?

"Maybe you could let me help you?" Angie's mouth curved into a kind of pathetic smile.

Rylee wanted her mother's influence in the shop about as much as she wanted to roll around in poison ivy. A sad smile cut up one side of her mouth. "I really have to go, Mom."

Chapter Twelve

After taking the time to visit with his father, which was a misnomer considering Pop slept for the entire time he was there, Darius sat with Toni in the finance department to discuss state-run facilities. She took her time to bring up websites, and he was amazed at how good the places tended to look. But after seeing that place in Madison, he knew better. Their website had shown a beautiful country estate with a smiley, happy person everywhere, which was nothing, nada, zip, like the sorry-assed place he had visited.

Time had gotten away from him, and he hoped he hadn't missed his chance to check out some of the stores in Sycamore River's downtown, Rosie's Bridals in particular, where he hoped he could glean some contact information. So far, he'd left several messages on the store's phone as well as on their website with no response. This place couldn't be a dead end.

Darkness had already descended, and the traffic around the town square was heavy. The congestion reminded him of the roadway rerouting he'd read about in the local rag. He could help one of these stores. He knew it. A new kind of fire burned in him today. Yes, this was about keeping his job, but, too, his mission could help the place where his roots grew. For the first time in a while, he remembered why he'd gotten into this business in the first place.

95

Although the bridal shop seemed the ideal candidate, securing the business for his show was a long shot, considering the owner just died. As he walked through the center of town, he spotted the florist that had been there forever, closed now that it was past five o'clock. The window was chock-full with Valentine's Day flower arrangements, balloons, and cupid cutouts on the window. *Wirth More* was not needed here. He walked on.

He strode beyond the theatre building and the library, places he'd frequented all during his growing up. He thought of matinees when he was a kid and pouring through the shelves of books with his mom in tow. The sandwich shop on a corner looked ordinary in a ham-and-cheese-on-hard-roll kind of way. He peered in the window. Closed up for the night, it appeared to be in decent shape, clean enough, with plenty of seating and a varietal menu up on the wall above the counter. Darius took out his cell phone and snapped a picture of the storefront of Mack's Midtown Deli. It could be a contender if someone else besides Mack ran the place.

A tuxedo store came into view. Not female friendly unless it was owned and operated by a woman or two or three. He snapped a photo of it just in case.

****

Rylee stood under the streetlight in front of Rosie's Bridals. She eyed the homemade sign she'd affixed to the front window. She couldn't decide if the poster board was crooked or if the slant was in her printing that stated the store would reopen soon. *Soon!* Was she crazy? How soon was soon? She had a sudden urge for chocolate, the kind that didn't melt in your hand. Just looking at the place, knowing it was hers, knowing the key in her pocket belonged to her caused a hitch in her chest. Exciting and intimidating at the same time.

"Hi," someone said from somewhere behind her.

She startled at the sound in the darkness. It was him. The pirate in the leather jacket. How could this keep happening unless God was just moving those chess pieces of his willy-nilly? Did he have a new game partner in Rosie Mandanello?

"Hi." It popped from her mouth like a question. What was he doing here?

"I keep running into you." He shook his head as if he himself couldn't figure out how it kept happening.

"Yeah," she said. *So lame.* She was capable of responding with more than one syllable, but she was still too enrapt in the way the street lamp illuminated his shiny black Superman hair.

"I, uh, was just down the block checking out that tuxedo place, Tuxedo Express."

Rylee's mouth went dry. Envisioning this man in a tuxedo was tough and unrelenting. A perfect fit to his frame, a white shirt crisp, the black satin tie undone. *Jeez.*

"Oh." Maybe he was getting married. Why should that bother her? Only a crazy person would lament a stranger's being off the market.

"Know anything about the place, like who runs it or anything?"

An odd question but she needed to answer if only to prove she could say an entire sentence. "They've been around a while, at least a decade I'd say, and the only thing I know is that some of our brides have used them, but beyond that I have no details."

"Your brides?" His forehead scrunched as he asked

the question.

"Oh." She chuckled. "Yeah." She pointed to the storefront behind him. "My bridal shop." It felt funny, almost like a lie to tell someone, a stranger, that this was *her* bridal shop. A little jiggle of delight coursed through her veins that felt pretty good as well.

He studied the awning. "You own Rosie's Bridals." He snapped his head around and stared, wide-eyed. "I'll be damned."

"Excuse me?" What an odd comment. Why would he be damned at the idea of her being the proprietor of Rosie's Bridals? Did she look as much of an imposter as she suddenly felt? The jiggle of delight she'd felt a moment ago evaporated like fog over a cooling pond.

"Uh, I read somewhere that the owner, an older woman, recently passed away."

"My grandmother."

"Oh. My condolences."

"Thank you." *Don't be nice. Just don't.*

"So you're going to be running the place?"

Defiance resurged with the same zapping of her breath she'd experienced at her mother's incredulity. "I am."

"Can I get you a cup of coffee?"

A cough of a laugh came to her lips. "Again? Because it went so well the first time?"

He laughed. Darius Wirth had a nice laugh, genuine sounding and odd coming from the pirate that he appeared to be. But, no, she should not have coffee with him. The part of her that was impulsive, the part that had gotten her into lots of trouble, wanted to have coffee with the pirate and share a croissant too, maybe. Feed him, even. *Stop!*

"Yes, there's something I'd like to talk to you about."

"Like?" She was stalling. What could he possibly want to talk to her about? It had something to do with her shop, obviously, but what? Maybe he really was getting married—why did that make her heart suddenly squeeze?—and wanted to scope out a place for his beloved fiancé to obtain her dress. *Yeah, that could be it.* "Are you in the market for a wedding gown?"

That laugh again. *Oh, Darius Wirth, please don't be delighted by me or anything I say.* This man couldn't know she was just off a wrong-guy relationship. He couldn't see her raw nerves or know how exposed they were, like open wires ready for one touch to ignite them. So this charmer needed to stop. Stop that handsomeness. And he could stop smelling so good too, if he knew what was good for both of them.

"In one way, yes, but not how you'd imagine."

A cross-dresser. *Oh, please be a cross-dresser.* "Okay, now you've got me curious."

"So what do you say? Jo-Jo's Java?"

She could very well assume that whatever he was selling, she wasn't or shouldn't be buying. She could walk away from this appealing pirate. Hasta la vista. But, nope.

"Okay." Before she could even think twice, she fell into step beside Darius Wirth in the bomber jacket, and they walked in sync to the coffee shop where she and her raw nerves almost couldn't wait to explode. That was just how crazy she was.

****

This Rylee would be a tough sell. Darius knew that with each step toward the coffeehouse. She and her

99

long, blue-jean-clad legs kept pace as they walked. The silence between them only served to conjure a cacophony of thoughts in his head. She wouldn't even graciously accept a payment for her coffee the other night. She sure as hell didn't seem like someone who would jump at the chance of having a stranger, one she obviously had developed a leeriness toward, to come into her shop and mess with it for the sake of television. But there was gold in that little run-down-looking store with the faded stripes on its awning and the rusted hinges on the front door.

He was paid handsomely to notice such things and turn them around, to make businesses hum, thrive, become the best they could be. And already he was summing up what the little shop needed aesthetically. But that was the easy part compared to convincing this girl with the swingy brown ponytail and the chin she was quick to jut in his face that he was the answer to what she needed.

He sneaked a glimpse. She was definitely nice looking, with a hot silhouette, but it was her spunk, the way she eyed him dismissively, untrustingly, her pretty face in a scrunch of attitude, that intrigued him. Frankly, not many women were so unimpressed with him. Most women fawned, if he were honest.

It wasn't boastful to think such a thought. It was true. He owned a mirror; he knew he'd inherited his mother's looks. Hell, it was one of the reasons the network had signed him. They'd called his looks "exotic," which was kind of ridiculous because there was nothing exotic about him. But the audience liked him, according to all the polls and the research done by the network. A man's man, Darius had found it easy working with the business owners from the earlier episodes. But those choices in businesses needed a change. Change or get the axe.

"Ladies, first," he said with a deliberate coat of charm as he opened the door to Jo-Jo's.

Rylee flashed him a give-me-a-break kind of look from her cool-looking eyes. Yeah, this Rylee McDermott was not so much impressed with him. However, tonight over a cup of caramel macchiato, his memory served him well. He would see if she was the answer to his problem.

****

Rylee sat at a table in the cozy coffeehouse, surrounded by the rich smells of ground beans. She studied her fingers as they cradled the warm ceramic mug. Darius Wirth hadn't even asked her what she'd like. Instead, he went to the counter and ordered her caramel macchiato with a shot of extra caramel. She wished she'd been irritated that he'd taken it upon himself to assume her beverage of choice. Instead, though, something tugged low in her belly. She was having an out-of-body experience. She watched the way her hands moved gently as they brought the hot drink to her lips. She took a sweet sip and savored the way it warmed its way through her on this chilly night. So cozy.

If she would have bet that she'd ever be here with Darius Wirth, she'd have lost. And it was kind of surreal to think that just days ago she sat across from Freddie in a dimly lit room, hoping and praying he was not going to get on one knee in the middle of the fine restaurant and propose marriage. *Ha.* Could she read people any more incorrectly?

She let her gaze filter to the man opposite her, who was quiet as he ran a finger over the rim of his mug. Round and round. That was one hypnotic fingertip. He had nice hands. Although she didn't want to think such thoughts or notice such things, the truth was that she was painting a picture of him in her head. She couldn't help it.

"So." She had to break the string of counterproductive thoughts that zipped around in her head like Pac-Man gobbling up her common sense. "What did you want to talk to me about?"

"Do you know who I am, Rylee?"

She swallowed the sarcasm that came to her mind and tried to make its way to her lips. No. She dared not give him a bit of her famous "lip," as her mother used to call it. Because of the way her body and her eyeballs were reacting to him, there was a very good chance anything that came out of her mouth would turn into a kind of flirtation, and that would be just stupid. He'd probably laugh at such a thing.

"Why don't you tell me who you are?"

"Have you ever seen the show on Living Loud TV called *Wirth More?*"

"I don't watch much TV."

"Okay." He pulled a little smile. "I'm the host of the show. We help businesses that need some guidance in getting to their, um, potential. Getting new businesses off the ground, steering already up-and-running establishments to meet their challenges. You know, such as what happens when a business changes hands."

"Like my bridal shop." So this was it. She couldn't explain the sudden stab of disappointment that hurt her midsection. What did she think this was, a date? Nope. This was just one more nonbeliever in the string of folks who didn't think she could run a bridal shop all by her lonesome. She sat up straighter. "I'm not into becoming anybody's guinea pig. Sorry."

"I read an article on your grandmother. She was the original owner of the store, am I correct?"

She took another long pull of her coffee and plunked the mug down onto the table. She wasn't going to discuss this with him. The last thing she needed was for somebody to swoop in and find out all that was wrong with Rosie's Bridals, especially this pirate of a guy.

"Yes, my grandmother owned and operated Rosie's Bridals for more than forty years. I'm looking forward to continuing the legacy of the place. So, again, I'm not interested in being on your TV show. Thank you for the coffee, though." She pushed back her chair.

"Wait." He reached across the table. His fingers rested on the cuff of her jacket. The touch was unpressured, but it weighed on her somehow. She studied the etched silver ring on his right hand. It was classy looking, not overstated, but a definite statement nonetheless.

She pinned him with her gaze, hoping he'd take the hint to remove his charming hand from her coat sleeve. However, her mouth went dry when she met his eyes, black like the surface of a lake at midnight. Lakes at midnight were dangerous, and jumping into them was just lunacy, but right now something whirred in her at the thought of being swallowed in those eyes.

"I didn't mean to insult you in any way, if that's what you're feeling." His voice was warm and laced with a tone of contrition. Had he practiced that tenor? Probably. He was in TV, and the convenient apology was that good.

She shrugged. "Not a problem. I am just not interested in your TV show. That's all. But, um, thank you for, you know, thinking of us."

"Would you do me one favor?"

With that hand still resting on her jacket sleeve, she could think of a couple of favors she could do for him, yes indeed, but God help her, she slowly slid her arm away from his touch and let her hands rest in her lap where they belonged.

"Will you watch an episode of the show? You can get it on demand. And then make a decision if you'd like to discuss this with me further?"

"I'm pretty busy."

"I know. I saw the sign in the window. A free bit of advice, Rylee. Don't jump the gun on the reopening. Better to get it right. "

Insecurity came flooding back, pelting her with questions and doubt. And for some reason, his mentioning the storefront notice was too personal, an invasion into her tender new game plan. Her feelings made no sense. The sign she'd posted was clearly marked on the front window of the store for anyone, the world, to see. Yet, this conversation delivered a flush to her skin with an intimacy she could not explain. And the way he said her name. Hypnotic. She liked it. Darius Wirth was dangerous for a sap like her.

She stood and for good measure, shoved her hands into her jacket pockets. "I'll take that under advisement. Thank you for the coffee. Again."

Darius stood. He wasn't quite six feet tall, she

guessed, but he was broad, fit—a manly pirate, for sure. And the way the collar of his nut-brown jacket was turned up, the shock of hair that refused to stay in place but rather take residence on his brow, well, it was nearly irresistible, and she wondered how many women could attest to the allure of this man.

He extended his hand. "Thanks for listening."

Unable to be rude thanks to her grandmother's constant rearing while she was growing up, she slipped a hand out from her jacket pocket and wished like hell she'd worn gloves. She accepted his warm hand into hers, and he gave it a gentle yet firm shake. But her skin liked his skin. Her fingers liked his fingers. Her palm squeezed closer inside his palm. She pulled away slowly, her finger pads sensitive as they trailed over his skin. She did her best to quell the rush of heat in her veins, the quickening in her chest, the clear and irrefutable *zoom*. This was nuts.

"You're welcome," she managed. A long, awkward pause hung heavy in the air as she breathed herself down from the steeplechase going on in her insides. Besides, she'd probably never see him again after this. Even though in the last several days they'd crossed paths three times, that was probably the limit of chance meetings. Bad things happened in threes is how the saying went.

"Please watch an episode." He gave her a smile, a melty kind of butter-on-a-griddle smile.

"No promises."

Darius Wirth held her gaze. "Good night, Rylee."

Before she did anything further to complicate her thoughts and her already disheveled life, Rylee turned and left Jo-Jo's, scrunched her shoulders up to her ears to combat the cold night, and stomped her way to Kit's apartment on Farragut Place.

Chapter Thirteen

When Kit opened her door, she was quite the sight in her oversized man's pinstriped pajamas and her hair bunched up on her head. "Hey," she said, her face quizzical.

Rylee recognized that look in her friend's eyes. Kit was worried. Those big round orbs of hers were locked on Rylee's face.

"Come on in."

"Thanks." Rylee stepped in and let her eyes scan the small, tidy room. She ran a hand through her hair and breathed evenly to quell an antsy urge to jump out of her own skin. Maybe caffeine at this hour hadn't been a great idea. She was full of not-so-great ideas.

"Can I get you something?"

"Anything potent."

"I have white wine and almond liquor."

Rylee studied her for a moment. "I'll have some of the white wine. Thanks."

She followed Kit into the kitchen cubicle, which was the best way to describe the square little space. Still, it was cute with its greenery on the windowsill and the copper-bottomed pans hanging from a wrought-iron rack.

Kit handed her a glass of wine and poured one for herself. She tilted her head in contemplation. "Come on. Let's go sit."

In the living room Kit positioned herself on the sofa. She began tentatively. "Something about the store?"

Rylee put her wineglass down on the coffee table and placed her hands on her hips. She looked up at the ceiling and blew out a lungful of air. "This has been one weird-assed night."

"Oh boy. Tell me."

"I suck at men. Irrefutable, right?" When Kit didn't respond, Rylee plopped down on the sofa beside her. "I'm looking for you to agree with me here, Kit. Okay?"

Kit shrugged while she took a sip from her glass. "We all do to some degree, friend. Men are tricky."

"No, really, I'm not exaggerating. I fail at the whole thing. Picking them, reading them. Especially reading them. Which brings me to the point of why I'm here."

"Are we going to need a refill?" Kit held up her dwindling drink.

"Bring the bottle."

While Kit poured, Rylee reiterated the news of Darius Wirth and his television show and, especially, his inquiry regarding Rosie's Bridals.

"So he's a television personality, your pirate." Kit nodded as if that made sense.

"Yes. He's not *my* anything. I've never heard of his show, though. Have you?"

"*Wirth More*. No, but that's easily remedied."

"He said it's on demand."

"Well, come on, then."

Kit pointed the remote at the television, and while surfing through numerous screens, she uttered a triumphant "voilà."

They watched in silence. Watched and sipped their wine. Darius looked good on screen, but that was no surprise. Each time he looked into the camera lens, his eyes piercing as though the conversation were a private one just between the two of them, a zing of heat charged through her. Maybe it was stress or the wine she was drinking, but suddenly she felt herself morphing back into an eighth-grader as her brain began tacking on a ridiculous *in bed* to everything he said. "Let me show you how this works *in bed.* The renovation will bring you plenty of action *in bed.* Now, this is how we create success *in bed.*" She was morphing into an eighth-grader minute by minute. She could almost feel a zit brewing on her chin.

The episode involved a pizzeria somewhere in New York. The place had been struggling with local competition, the area saturated with other pizza shops. *Wirth More* went in and helped them revitalize their menu options, gave them ideas on a new look for the interior of the place, everything black and white with touches of red. The transformation was pretty dramatic. By the end of the episode, the owners of Brothers' Pizza happily announced business was up and their customers raved about the new menu choices. *Wirth More* made Brothers' Pizza just that—worth more.

They watched a second episode, this one involving a tackle-and-bait shop somewhere in Ocean County. It had been a top spot, according to the episode, until Superstorm Sandy ravaged the area. Now Bait This was struggling to hold on for dear life. And the swashbuckling Darius Wirth swooped in as big as day to rescue the fledgling little store.

109

By the end of the episode, Bait This was back on track. The store got a facelift, new paint, new counters, and an endorsement from some big-shot rod-and-reel manufacturer. There were new displays, ongoing promotions, and before they knew it, the little place was jammed, and according to the final voice-over, they were on the road to big things—*in bed. Oh God.*

Kit aimed the remote at the screen, and with a push of a button, the screen went black. "What are your thoughts?" She turned to Rylee and finished her wine.

"I told him no. Actually, I told him I'd consider watching an episode. So I did, and it's still no."

"Are you sure about that?" Kit leaned closer. "Did you hear what they said? If they pick your business, they give you ten grand for renovations and marketing and stuff. Ten thousand dollars, Rylee."

"I know, but so?" Rylee stood and walked over to the little bistro table at the other side of the room. She set her wineglass down. "I don't want to be paraded all over the world as some kind of loser who needs Superman to swoop in and save the day."

"He kind of does look like Superman, you know, if Superman were a conquistador."

"Irrelevant." Rylee folded her arms.

"True. But let's look at this for a second. We don't know how Rosie's Bridals is going to fare once we open. I mean, everyone was used to Rosie herself, right? That was one of your arguments to me when I was trying to convince you to reopen. Who's to say that this show couldn't help make things even better for business?"

"Kit, I can't. It's too much. With all the naysayers around me, I'm overwhelmed as it is. I can't even imagine what it would be like to have *him* all up in my face."

Kit wagged an accusatory finger. "Is this about him? Not the show. The man?"

Rylee flashed her a look. "Um, hello. I'm still reeling from Freddie being a turd."

"Let's put it this way, friend. Don't let whatever hesitations you have with this specimen of manhood make you kick a gift horse right smack dab in the face."

"I can't believe I'm the one saying this, but have some faith. You'll see." Rylee pinned on a smile she did not feel. "Who needs Darius Wirth?"

Chapter Fourteen

While Jake eyeballed him over the rim of his coffee cup, Darius reiterated Saturday night's serendipitous meeting with the young woman named Rylee McDermott.

"The girl with the coffee." It wasn't a question. It was a statement, and it was tinged with Jake's particular brand of disdain.

"Her name is Rylee McDermott."

"So you've said." Jake scratched his head. "I've seen her on YouTube."

"And don't bring up that video somebody sent to you. She wasn't acting crazy that night. She was, I don't know, embarrassed or something."

"Well, her business is ideal. A bridal shop." Jake tilted his head. "Parker Paper will love it."

"That was my thought." Darius needed to convince Rylee McDermott to be on board with the show. He neglected to reiterate her emphatic *thanks, but no thanks.* He wasn't taking that for an answer.

"How soon can you clinch the deal?"

Darius's cell phone sounded with a message alert. He tapped the screen and read the text from Toni at The Memory Center. They'd arranged appointments at two state-run nursing homes for Darius to visit this week. She moved the appointments up a day because of an iffy snow forecast. Time was running short there too.

"Jake, I've got to head back to Sycamore River tomorrow to work on my father's nursing home situation. Afterward I can contact Rylee and work on a commitment."

"Do that. But hope you know there's a snowstorm brewing out over the Atlantic, and according to Al Roker, if system A meets system B, it could be a whopper."

Darius had been so focused on the show and his father's situation that he'd known nothing about the forecast. "That's what this text was about. When's it expected?"

"Sometime in the next forty-eight hours."

"Shit. It better stay out of my way. I've got things to do."

"Better tell that to Al."

Chapter Fifteen

Rylee and Kit worked nonstop at the store. The labor only served to fuel her resolve to make this work. Screw Darius Wirth and his TV show. Bad choice of thought. *Screw* and *Darius* should not be in the same sentence. The phrase could fuel all kinds of images.

Freda and Mary Ann came by, wanting to help, so together the four women went over the interior of the store with a fine-tooth comb. They cleaned, they washed, and they polished. They helped Rylee with a list of reps from dress designers for when she'd place orders for the new line. Dress selection was the scariest part of all because finding the right samples from the best designers to exemplify the new look and feel of Rosie's Bridals was key.

By Wednesday, news of a nor'easter on the fringes of northern New Jersey was everywhere. No matter where she went, people were abuzz. Her mother had done a big food shop and came by the apartment with an armload of staples. What she thought Rylee needed with a five-pound bag of flour and a pillow-sized bag of dry lentils was beyond her.

Angie looked around the apartment. The changes Rylee had made were subtle ones, yet it still made her feel judged to have Angie cast her gaze at the new striped toss pillows on the sofa, the rearrangement of the side chairs, the absence of the tablecloth on the dining table.

They went into the kitchen where things were different as well. New dish drainer, Rylee's pod coffeemaker on the counter, a new toaster, blinds on the window where frilly curtains had been. Angie's gaze flitted over everything, pausing at the apple-peeling device affixed to the counter. Rylee hadn't had the heart to remove it.

"How do you like the place?" she asked as she unloaded the items from the brown paper bags. Enough carrots to feed a world of rabbits, a bag of potatoes, some spiky-looking herb in a plastic pouch. Ah, and a bottle of chardonnay. *Go, Angie!*

"You've made some nice changes, honey." A rueful smile claimed Angie's mouth. "Rosie would approve."

Rylee's heart skipped a beat. "You think so?"

"I do."

Angie was subdued today. Maybe her mood stemmed from being inside the place that used to belong to Rosie. Suddenly, Rylee felt a stab of guilt. Maybe she should have left everything the way it was. Did every change serve as a swipe of an eraser? What kind of granddaughter was she not to think of that before?

"Thanks, uh, for all this, Mom." She tried to lighten the mood, forced her mouth into an upward curve. "Not sure what I'm supposed to do with everything."

"Make soup, of course." Angie brightened. "My famous lentil soup. I can help you, if you want."

Now that Angie was Zen and now that she was happily partnered with the earthy Sonny who showed her the bliss of creating things from your own hands, she had become a fan of homemade soups, particularly a legume aficionado. The woman loved soaking beans, dumping them in a pot with handfuls of this and that, and conjuring a big, aromatic pot of hearty and oh-so fiber-rich love.

Lentil soup was good stuff, true, and Rylee guessed that in light of the weather forecast, it was a natural choice for Zen Angie to bring her the ingredients. And today, with the way that look had come over her mother's face when her eyes catalogued the differences in the apartment above Rosie's Bridals, Rylee had one choice.

"Yes," she said. "Show me how you make lentil soup."

****

By the time all the ingredients were bubbling in the pot, the snow had started. It came down in small flakes, rapid and steady, the kind of snow that meant business, not the fat, lazy type of flakes that sometimes floated down from the sky more for show than anything else. By four o'clock it was dark as night.

"I'd better get home. Sonny will be out looking for me." Angie, with the prideful smile of one who had a partner anxious for their return, was back to herself. *Namaste.*

"Thanks for the soup, Mom." An odd twinge flittered in her chest. In thirty years mom and daughter had never performed a dual soup project, and it was nice and weird both.

"Maybe I can't make pie, but man, can I do soup or what?" Angie grinned.

"You have enough for you and Sonny?"

Angie held up a plastic container. "More than enough."

When Angie was wrapped in the cape thingy that she'd manufactured on her own loom, black with a white- and burnt-orange Aztec-looking border, she donned an oversized hat and her homemade mittens and carried her container of soup to the door.

Rylee peered out to the street at the frosty-white dusting on the road and walkways. "You okay to drive?"

"It's just a couple blocks, honey bun," Angie said. She touched a woolen-clad hand to Rylee's cheek. "You call me if you need anything. We might be snowed in for a while."

"I'll be fine, Mom. Going to spend the next day or so going through more of the mail, seeing where things are with the store."

"Off I go, then." Angie trotted herself to her car.

****

Darius hated both the Mountain View Nursing Home in the far reaches of Morris County and the more local Primrose Manor in Denville. Each had appeared decent enough on the outside, but once he'd walked into the patient areas, the sour air assaulted his nostrils like an open-handed slap.

In the short time he'd been searching for a new home for his father, he'd learned how to scrutinize the candidates. Was the staff engaged? Did any of the offerings on the food trays look the least bit edible? Did the patients seem cared for, clean, attended to? Nothing compared to The Memory Center, and it pained him that his father couldn't stay there.

Back at The Memory Center, he first went to see

Toni to let her know his findings. After a back-and-forth with her regarding the ticking clock and the snow halting the search for alternatives, they made the decision to add Pop to the list to be moved to Mountain View, the least offensive facility he'd seen so far.

"I'm going to stop in to see my father and then head out." He offered his hand to Toni. "Thank you again for all your help."

"Gladly." A warm smile came to her lips. "Remember this storm's not letting up anytime soon. Safe home, okay?"

"Sure thing."

Darius took the elevator up to his father's room, where he found the old man asleep on his side, the blankets up to his chin. Was it cold by the window? He went over to the glass panes and tested the air with his hand. The window was right above the heater, so no, it wasn't cold there. His father looked grumpy when he slept, always had. His brow tended to scrunch in on itself, and his mouth pulled down in an exaggerated arc. The old man was dreaming. His eyeballs darted back and forth under parchment-paper lids, and his brittle body jerked in conjunction with the movements. What was going on in that foggy brain of his? His heart squeezed. He did not want to move Pop from this place. He wished he could just let the old man be.

He took a tentative step closer and touched a light hand to his father's head, smoothing the flyaway white hair.

His father murmured at the touch. "Arabella."

Always. Martin Wirth, regardless of his ability to know the day or the year or to recognize the face of his only son, would always call for his wife.

****

The snow was steady and coming down at an angle. Darius had thrown a few essentials into a bag and called to book himself a room at the chain hotel right near The Memory Center. It was just another reason to like the place, having a pretty decent hotel adjacent to the facility for family and friends who needed a room. The snow was heavy and hit his face with an assaulting sting. It swirled at his feet as he made his way down the already-covered walkways in downtown. His heart, too, was heavy, and Pop's leaving The Memory Center assaulted his insides with the same sting of the snow in his face.

He stopped into Jabberwocky's for a whiskey. While he sipped his potent beverage, he pondered the woman with the determination in her eyes—Rylee MacDermott. Her business was an ideal one for his show, but she interested him too. Maybe it was the whiskey, but he couldn't get her out of his head. She was nothing like Caroline or the others he'd dated before her. Caroline had been one of those women with an agenda, and he'd felt like just one thing on her to-do list. Marry a man, have a baby, buy a house upstate.

He should have paid more attention. All the signs had been there from the start. He had been so wrapped up in making a name for himself he'd missed her campaigning, all that chatter about diamond shapes and the best months for weddings. Hindsight had made it clear. His silence had boded as compliance to the anxious Caroline.

The ultimatum came about a year ago, and like that, she was gone. Last he heard, she was engaged to a podiatrist. The news hadn't bothered him.

Suddenly, he thought of his dad's whimper tonight, calling for his Arabella. Maybe that's what Darius was looking for somewhere deep inside. Maybe he wanted to love a woman enough to be all in, to have her name the only name he could remember when he was an old man.

He finished his whiskey and ordered another. Rylee MacDermott. Yeah, she had a nice physical appeal, and under normal circumstances he'd probably ask her out to dinner or something. But tonight in the snow and the cold, whiskey on his lips, he wanted to talk to her. That's it. Just find out if she'd trust him to do right by her grandmother's bridal shop.

He guzzled the rest of his drink, paid his tab, zipped up his coat, and headed in the direction of Rosie's Bridals.

Chapter Sixteen

By seven o'clock Rylee's eyeballs were squirrely. The stack of mail was bottomless. The more she opened, the more appeared. Bills and more bills. She'd had no idea Rosie's wasn't as humming an establishment as she'd presumed. The water bill was two payments behind. The electric and gas were due, and she had no idea where the money would come from for those payments. And the taxes. The tax bill was a whopper. Was there really no cushion of money in some account somewhere to cover these bills? Had Rosie's Bridals been on the brink of a shutdown? Suddenly, she felt guilty for using what precious stash she'd had on frivolous throw pillows at the discount home-goods store and the new toaster from Target. At the moment she was broke as a joke.

She opened the bottle of chardonnay her mother had brought and decided to enjoy a bowl of the lentil soup. While she was pulling a soup bowl from a cabinet, her cell phone sounded and she grabbed the device and gave it a swipe.

"Rylee," a male voice spoke into her ear. She didn't need him to identify himself. She already knew. It was the pirate. "It's Darius Wirth."

"Hello." She took a pull of her wine. The wine slithered a smooth trail down her throat. Maybe the beverage would render her immune to the sound of his voice in her ear. She sipped again.

"Um, I know this is unorthodox, but can I talk with you?"

"Darius," she said, surprised at how saying his name gave her heart a giddy jump. "I've already told you I'm not interested in being part of your show."

"Ten minutes. Just give me ten minutes."

"Tonight?" She didn't want to see him or talk to him or smell him, for that matter. "We're in the middle of a snowstorm. I'm not going anywhere tonight."

"You don't have to. I'm downstairs."

"What?" She finished the wine in her glass. Oh, this was not good. Not good at all. She glanced down at her appearance—pink flannel lounge pants with black-and-white kittens all over them, a black sweatshirt with Got Wine? written across the chest, and multicolored striped slipper socks with rubber gripper thingies on the sole. Oh God. No way, Jose.

"Just ten minutes. No pressure. Just hear me out."

She could almost see his face—those chiseled cheekbones, the hair black like a crow's wing, flashing eyes like wet river stones. Why hadn't she thought to wear a cocktail dress tonight? *Okay, no.* She swallowed an expletive. *Quit messing with your own head, fool.*

Letting him inside her apartment would be crazy, considering she found him nearly irresistible in person. And now, reaching a new height in poor choices in regard to the male species, she couldn't resist the man's voice either. With another glance at her ridiculous getup, she hoped he'd take one look at her and keep his distance, the pajamas serving as a kind of shield of flannel.

"Come up the back staircase."

Chapter Seventeen

As he climbed the stairs and with each footfall of his booted feet, Rylee's mind chanted *shit, shit, shit* in time with his ascent.

He was soaked to the gills, his jacket dark with wetness, and his hair shimmery with facets of snow. *Oh boy. A wet pirate.* She waved a hand. "Come in."

Scrutinizing eyes did a sweep of her from head to toe, and although her insides stretched and pulled like Silly Putty, she willed her stupid getup to repulse him enough to stomp away.

Instead, though, the pirate said the unthinkable. "Cute outfit. Comfy looking for a night like this." His face had brightened before he'd said the words, and a kind of smirky, slanty, appealing little smile played on his lips. So much for a shield of flannel.

"I can't believe you came out on a night like this."

"Yeah. I was visiting my father at the nursing home up on Highland Avenue. I knew going back home to Hoboken on a train might get tricky, so I booked a room at a hotel. It's not far from here, and I can walk it back before it gets too deep out there."

Ten minutes. That's all she'd agreed to. Certainly, within ten minutes the sidewalks outside would still be navigable. *Let's get this over with.*

She pulled her gaze away and remembered her manners. "Here. Let me take your coat."

Darius shrugged out of his jacket, and she hooked it on the coat-tree by the door. The black woolen scarf slung around his neck only added to his appeal. He rubbed his hands together and gave a little shiver. "Wicked night."

"Okay, so what did you need to talk to me about on such a wicked night?"

He cast his eyes around the place, the dark orbs assessing and then landing on the counter where an empty bowl and spoon sat next to the large soup pot positioned on the stove. "Something smells good."

Rylee swallowed hard. "Um, yeah, it's soup."

"No better night for soup. What kind?"

"Lentil."

"Mmmm."

Okay, do not make sounds that a crazy woman could construe as a moan. Her heart did another Silly Putty push/pull.

Life had a way of putting choices in front of her. What was that old saying? Something about the same boneheaded problems presenting themselves until the lesson was finally learned? Well, she was a slow learner.

Her problem here tonight was with this wet, glistening pirate who impeded her from making a wise choice, her greatest flaw. Most of her decisions backfired with aftershocks that tended to spread across all things important. Like the weightiness of the bridal shop downstairs that waited for her rescue.

And at the moment, with this hunk of a man in her apartment looking all dark and mysterious with that brown sweater and the black woolen scarf at his neck, she glanced down at the empty wineglass in her hand

and let right and wrong be damned. "Would you like some wine?"

She needed a shrink and not more wine, but all she had was wine. Wine and soup and a pirate.

****

Darius hadn't expected this. Yeah, he'd found her kind of cute, even when she'd been a hot mess that first night at Jo-Jo's Java House. And tonight in that thirteen-going-on-thirty outfit, he found her nearly irresistible. It made no sense. He'd always been a little black dress, stiletto-heel fan. But here in her apartment he was taken with the girl despite of, or maybe even because of, the slack lounge pants and oversized sweatshirt.

Maybe it was just the whiskey he'd downed. He was here to pitch his show, and he needed to clinch the deal. Everything depended on it. He shook off the urge to flirt with her, the inclination niggling low in his belly.

Rylee poured measures of wine into two glasses while he seated himself on a stool at the small square butcher-block counter. He took a deep breath. "Thank you for agreeing to see me." He accepted the wine she slid in his direction, careful not to let his fingers touch hers. "And thanks for this too."

Keeping her distance at the opposite side of the island, Rylee MacDermott nodded and reached up to rumple her hair. She had great hair. A lush cascade of dark brown, smooth and sleek, and he imagined in summertime the sun would streak random strands gold or copper. His chest locked, and he willed himself to stop with the imaginings. By summertime this woman would be history to him. His need was now, and it was not about her. It was about the bridal shop.

"Let me ask you this, Rylee." He fiddled with the stem of the wineglass. "How soon do you expect to reopen your doors to the store?"

"I'm still getting used to the idea of having a store in the first place." She chuckled a nervous sound. "I've been going through mail, tying up some loose ends. You know, trying to get grounded. But none of this, as I said, compels me to sign on for national TV to come in and..." She stopped herself by taking a sip of her wine. "It's just not something I feel comfortable with."

"How about the financial contribution provided by the show? I'm sure you could use the ten grand we invest in your store."

Her gaze flitted across the room, and he followed it. A mountain of envelopes was stacked on one side of a small desk, and the trash can beside it brimmed with wadded paper. Rylee swallowed hard and gave her hair another toss with her hand.

"Well, yeah, who couldn't use ten thousand dollars? But seriously, I'm just not comfortable having cameras and, um, you hovering around here while I figure out what I'm doing."

Unable to look away from her eyes, he came to a conclusion. She was attracted to him. Despite that unimpressed look on her face, the jutted chin, the wary eyes, she felt the same tugging he did. Based on the clear message he read in her green eyes, that wasn't a good thing.

He filled his lungs with air, and the whoosh of release cleared his thoughts. If she wasn't attracted to him, she might be more interested in letting *Wirth More* help her. Different time, different place, he'd seize this moment. But not now. Not with all he had on the line.

"Look, I guarantee you'll be glad you signed on to do the episode. We tape on Wednesdays, Thursdays, and Fridays. Each day we're on site about six hours—"

"Six hours?"

That quick jab of a comment convinced him he had more work to do. "It goes by quickly. You'll see. First off, though, I'd go over your financials with you. Find out the status of things."

"No way." She sipped her wine. "Are you kidding? No way."

"That part wouldn't be televised, Rylee. That would be between the two of us. I need to know where the store stands so I can figure out how best to help it."

She lifted her wineglass again and closed her lips over the rim, tilting her head back for another taste. The pulling sensation ignited low in his belly. He closed his eyes to regroup. He had some wine. "Look, it works like this. On Monday you and I meet with the production team and go over the paperwork." Those green eyes of hers filled with a big *hell no,* but he barreled on as if he hadn't seen it. "It's just a simple contract stating you allow me and my crew to film the episode. Later that day and the next, I do an assessment of the store. We, you and I, decide how best to use the ten grand. We film the next three days, and our part is done. The editing and all that stuff takes place without us."

She was quiet, her mouth quirked up on one side.

"So how about it, Rylee? Who kicks a gift pirate in the mouth?"

"Ha-ha." She turned her attention to the pot on the stove. She sank a ladle into the soup and stirred. Lifting her gaze to meet his, she bit down on the pillow of her lower lip. "Would you like some soup?"

"Sure," he said, feeling a twinge of success.

****

Rylee stood on her side of the island while she tasted the soup, watching Darius lift his spoon to his mouth. His lips closed over the bowl of the spoon, and she was riveted to the business of his swallow—the Adam's apple bobbing, the tip of his tongue darting out to lick his lower lip. *Zoom.* Holy mackerel, she was so screwed. Her mind roiled with the decision at hand. Could she really walk away from ten thousand dollars when all those unpaid bills mocked her from across the room?

Oh, Rosie, how'd you get me into this predicament?

On the other hand, filming the show would take just a week. One stinking, lousy week and then he and his reality show would be gone from her world. And she'd be on the other side of panic with the financing of Rosie's Bridals. Could she do it? Could she stand it?

"Ask me any questions, Rylee." He spooned more soup. "This is great, by the way. You make it from scratch?"

"With my mom." She laughed and shook her head.

"Why's that funny?"

"Let me put it this way. My mom and I don't typically do things together. We're more like tugging on the opposite ends of a rope." She poured more wine into his glass and then her own. *Holy smokes, he was cute.*

When his bowl was empty, he wiped his mouth with a napkin. "Thank you for that. It hit the spot." He lifted his wineglass. "And for the wine. Good thing I'm not driving."

"Holy mackerel." Rylee dashed to the window. "I forgot all about the snow." She peered out the glass pane. The sidewalk was virtually invisible under a white fluffy blanket. *Oh God.* She had to get this guy out of here.

"How is it out there?" He got up from the stool and came around to her side of the room and stood next to her to peer out the window. "Wow."

"Yeah." She turned to face him. She hadn't realized how close he was, and her heart was a lone sock in a dryer—flapping around and around in her chest. "You, uh, think you can get to the hotel in this?"

His mouth curved up on one side, and his eyes twinkled "If I leave right now."

It was odd how relief and disappointment careened around in her chest at the same time. Two trapped bumblebees zipped around, chasing one another.

"Let me get your coat." She all but ran to the coatrack by the door.

Darius pulled on his coat, and while his hand tugged a lazy path with the zipper, he cocked his head and flashed her an inquisitive look. "So, Rylee MacDermott, you weren't too keen on my buying you that cup of coffee that day. But will you let me help Rosie's Bridals?"

And like that, one bumblebee in her chest killed the other one and zoomed a victory lap around her ribs. "I'd meet with the people from the show on Monday?"

"Yes. I'll be there as well."

As if that were any comfort. She had to be a big girl and do this for her grandmother's shop. There was a

M. Kate Quinn

reason the old woman put it in her hands. She had
believed Rylee could rescue it. So she would. "Yes,
then. I'm in."

"That's great." He touched a hand to her arm. "You
won't be sorry."

She already was, but that was beside the point. The
shop, the money, and Rosie's legacy were more
important than this guy's ability to make her *zoom*.

At the open door he turned to her. "Thank you."

She couldn't respond. She couldn't even swallow.

"For trusting me to help your shop. I'm already
getting the idea how much it must mean to you."

Her insides flooded with heat. This guy was
reading her, and she felt naked. Her right hand floated
up and gripped her left shoulder. An arm shield.

"Oh, and thanks for the wine and the soup too."

"You're, uh, welcome."

"Maybe it's the alcohol talking, but I'm curious
about something." He gave her a half smile. "What
made you decide that I resemble a pirate?"

Heat bathed her face, and things inside her body
thumped. A drum beat. A rhythm she wanted to dance
to.

After a hard swallow, she managed a shrug. "I
don't know. The face, I guess, and, uh"—she waved her
fingers at him—"probably that hair of yours." Too
much wine and too much thumping prevented her from
shutting the hell up. She wagged her index finger
toward his forehead. "And your, um, eyebrows, the way
they kind of arch like that." She pointed at his face.
"They're doing it now, as a matter of fact."

Darius stepped closer and gazed down into her
eyes. "Is that a good thing?"

She laughed because something had to fill the space between them. "I don't know."

He stepped closer still, his breath so close she could feel it on her face. He smelled of wine and the woods. His mouth was so near. That pillow of a lower lip all but had her name written on it.

"Well, maybe it's the wine," he said. "But I'm kind of flattered."

Thump. Thump. Zoom. "You are?" She tightened the grip on her shoulder.

"Yes."

"It, uh, was just an observation, really." The words trailed off into a whisper.

"But that's off the record."

Rylee swallowed hard and found her voice. "What do you mean off the record?"

Darius Wirth moved a step away and shoved his hands into his jacket pockets. "My producers and the sponsors frown on any involvement between the host and anyone associated with a business we're filming."

Heart stammering, she focused on the result, the *zoom* this pirate gave her be damned. So it was a godsend that the fine people at Living Loud TV had that rule. Maybe that would work better than her flannel pajama pants that were supposed to make them immune to each other.

"Oh."

"Yeah."

"That wouldn't be a problem whatsoever." She shook her head. "Not at all. None. Zip."

"Okay, good."

"Okay, good."

Chapter Eighteen

"Did you say you're going to be on TV?" Zen Angie's mouth gaped open. "Why? What'd you do?"

"I'm not going to be on *America's Most Wanted*," Rylee said. "Sit a minute. Let me give you the lowdown."

With her mother and Sonny's eyes locked on her face, she explained the situation. Periodically, the pair gave each other side-glances, clearly straining to keep their focus on Rylee.

"You see," Rylee piped in, "it makes all the sense in the world."

"Seems like it. And, wow, ten thousand dollars. That's a godsend." Sonny sounded enthusiastic, but that was him. Life was one big happy surprise to a guy like him.

Godsend. Rylee mulled over the word. A gift horse. Suddenly, an image of a dark stallion came to mind, the steed charging across a field, its muscles rippling, body glistening from exertion, mane whipping behind him. She had to stop thinking about Darius in any way other than the means to a ten-thousand-dollar end. No more old movies either. They had a way of tainting her view of reality. Darius Wirth was not *Flicka,* and he was not her *friend.*

Zen Angie slapped her knees with a familiar gesture. "Well, then," she uttered. It was her way of saying there was nothing she could do about her daughter agreeing to be on a reality television show. Which meant she thought Rylee was nuts, or rather that her daughter was once again making crazy decisions.

She'd prove her wrong. This one time. She would.

****

Her conversation with Kit went better. The two of them did an impromptu jig, arms around each other, right in the middle of the day inside Rosie's Bridals.

"Honestly, Kit, when I saw all the bills that need to be paid, I thought how the hell am I going to pull this off?"

"And think about this. The publicity for the shop is going to be big. I mean, *Wirth More* is nationally televised. You couldn't ask for a better situation. And the icing on the cake, of course, is working side by side with that hunky host. Every girl should have their very own pirate."

Rylee shook her head. "No, no. None of that, friend. Darius Wirth is strictly off limits."

"Says who?"

"Says him, for one. And the show execs apparently. No fraternizing with the little people, I guess."

"There's ways around that." Kit flashed a wicked grin. "When the episode's all wrapped up, you can keep company if you're so inclined, can't you?"

"No. It'll get back to the media, and it'll look biased or something. I don't know. But whatever, he's a no go."

"But if he weren't?" Kit smirked. "I suspect the guy makes you *zoom*."

Rylee returned the wicked grin. "Since we're just

talking *what if*, I'd ride him like a horse and put him in the barn wet."

Kit laughed with her mouth open, face turned up to the ceiling and hand clutched to her chest. "So is this what happens when a guy makes you *zoom*?"

"Yup. And leave it to me to *zoom* for a guy I can't go near."

"That's going to be a toughie."

Rylee took in the interior of the bridal shop, eyed all that needing doing. Despite their cleaning efforts, the place still looked kind of outdated. She thought of Rosie, whose pride in the place was undeterred. Rylee wouldn't ruin this opportunity with her girlish crush. Besides, Darius Wirth probably had a pack of women hot after him.

****

On Monday Rylee found herself in Hoboken in the reception room of Living Loud TV. The woman behind the desk fielded phone calls and periodically looked up from her task to give Rylee a reassuring smile. Her stomach was a clenched fist, and her lungs made of rock. Her hands in her lap gripped her purse as if it were a life raft and she were out at sea awaiting the coast guard to find her.

She let her gaze filter to the large wooden door to the left of the receptionist, which a woman carrying a stack of files stepped through. Was Darius in there already? Was there a premeeting going on in there? No matter how hard she tried to still her mind, she could not. It whipped around with regret, but she would not let the moment get to her. She couldn't. She had to do this.

****

"We're putting all our eggs in this basket, Darius. Are you sure this woman isn't a screwball? I mean, if the video that college kid sent me were to go viral, it could make us look like idiots."

"Jake, trust me. This is the business we need. A nice young woman who was bequeathed a bridal shop she has no idea how to keep afloat. It's a gift that landed right in our laps. Meet her and see. She's nice."

"You've said that already. I'm going to trust you, buddy, because time's up. After we meet with her, we'll report to Parker Paper that we're ready for production."

"Great. This will buy us a second season. You'll see."

"Because she's nice."

"Just meet her."

"Call her in."

****

Darius sat beside her while his boss, Jake Somebody, went over what to expect. He sounded matter of fact about how the camera crew would be up in her face, all over her life like a swarm of flies on roadkill. But it wouldn't be for long. The crew would be at Rosie's Bridals for three sessions, and then her part in the production would be done.

They wanted to start right away. Wednesday. Her heart did a flip. Didn't they say TV made people look heavier than they really were? Could she lose ten—no, twenty—pounds by Wednesday when this was already Monday? That was going to be a tough one, considering that all morning she couldn't wait to attack the bag of peanut M&M's in her purse. Oh God, what was she doing?

They all shook hands, and she was given a folder

of the paperwork Darius would go over with her in detail while he assessed the needs of her business in the coming days.

In no time she and Darius were alone in the room, a space too large for the sense of crowdedness that gripped her. *Get used to it.* There could be plenty of times in the coming days when she and Darius would be alone in a room. She took even breaths to still her mind, but each intake was teased with the piney scent of his cologne. She'd been wrong to expect relief when the meeting ended. This wasn't the end of her nervous breakdown. It was the beginning.

Chapter Nineteen

Jake came back into the conference room with his big, gratuitous smile painted on his face. "Will you excuse us a sec?" he said to Rylee.

She uttered a soft "sure" and headed for the door to the reception area. Her hair bounced as she walked and caught the glint of the overhead lights.

"I won't be long," Darius called after her.

After she left, Jake gave Darius's shoulder a fisted jab. "You were right about this one."

Not sure if this was Jake's typical sarcasm, he folded his arms and waited for more. He clenched his jaw.

"She's likeable enough, and we can use that wacky tendency she's got to our advantage. Play it up."

"What are you talking about? What wackiness?" His jaw ached.

"Come on, bro. Tell me you saw the way the coffee spoon fell out of her cup and she used her shirtsleeve to mop up the spill." Jake looked up at the ceiling, and a crack of laughter escaped from his throat. "You can't script this any better."

Darius blew out a lungful of air. "No, I didn't see that. But so what? She was nervous. That was all. Still not sure what you're getting at."

Jake slung an arm around his shoulder. "What I'm getting at, my thickheaded friend, is that the audience is going to love that she's imperfect, and our happy-ending bit will be smooth like butter."

Darius never liked the part of the show Jake dubbed the "happy-ending bit." Yeah, it made for better drama, but it was always at the expense of the store owner's nerves. The time they deliberately had the cardboard companies deliver the wrong-size pizza boxes for Brothers' Pizzeria nearly sent the eldest brother to the hospital with palpitations. The ploy worked for the show's sake, true, but Darius didn't like it, and somehow pulling a deliberate prank like that on Rylee pissed him off.

"What happy-ending bit are you talking about, Jake?"

"Oh, we'll think of something. Don't worry."

****

Before she knew it, Rylee was driving Darius to Rosie's Bridals. His presence beside her in the car squeezed her insides. His nearness drew gooseflesh over her body, like being trapped with her own worst nightmare. Just inches away sat a guy she wanted to put her hands on and yet was forbidden to touch. *Where was tequila when you needed it?*

Luckily, he carried the conversation, asking her questions about what she envisioned for the store, what were its greatest needs. All business. And to contradict him was the scent of his woodsy cologne that might as well have been blowing kisses at her.

At the shop they sat together at Rosie's desk and went over the paperwork. She'd been almost afraid to use the calculator to tally what she owed for utilities and creditors. Why hadn't Rosie talked to her, or anyone as far as she knew, about the arrearages? To her dying day, Rosie had been the sweet, smart woman with the indelible smile ready for every single would-be bride who graced her shop.

"You doing okay?" Darius asked. His shoulder met hers, and she nudged away from his warmth.

Rylee looked up from the paperwork and blew out a breath. "Yeah, but it's a lot. You know?"

His dark eyes shone with understanding. "It is. Does it make you feel uncomfortable going through all this with me? Like I told you, the particulars are not for the viewing audience. When we film this part, it will be just us shuffling through paperwork we've already made decisions about. Okay?"

"Okay."

He tapped her shoulder again, and she wished he wouldn't touch her. She liked it, and considering he was a total no go, that brief meeting of their shoulders, even through thick sweaters, was a thrill and then a lament—as if she'd bought herself a bag of her favorite candy and had managed to misplace it.

After going over the store's needs, they formulated a plan to divvy the stipend among the most pressing bills, some sprucing up of the interior, and new sample dresses for the upcoming season.

"I've come up with a plan for an open house. How do you feel about that?"

Rylee gave a nod. "Sure, that would be great. But what does that involve?" She had the feeling that she was rolling down a hill with no brakes.

"First off, the trick will be to get those sample dresses ordered soon so you'll have them ready for the open house. A fashion show of the new styles. The show will provide the models. I'm thinking next

Saturday. The crew and I will come back to film the event like a grand finale. A closure for our show's season and the beginning of your new version of Rosie's Bridals. Nice?"

"It sounds great, but I'm not sure I can order dresses and get them in time." What the hell did she know about those timeframes? The sales consultants would know better than she.

"Can we do a conference call with your sales staff?" His eyes were intense and, frankly, imposing.

When he looked like that, she could truly imagine him at the helm of a ship, patch over an eye, a ragged-edged shirt exposing his pecks. *Oh my God.* She squeezed her eyes shut. How was she supposed to do business with this Errol Flynn of a man? And why had she watched all those old movies with her grandmother? Now they were seared in her brain, and Darius was fracturing her memories of the old flicks.

Before she knew it, the sun was setting and darkness seeped into the space.

"I can't believe it's almost five o'clock." Darius rubbed his eyes. "Let's call it a day."

Rylee reached past him and switched on the desk lamp. She would not, could not, sit alone in the dark with this man. Uh-uh.

"I think we got a lot done today, Rylee. Your job is to order gowns with your sales team. Do that in the morning and promise them your firstborn if you have to, but get them delivered here before next Saturday. The funds will be deposited into your account. You can clean up the bills, and I'll be back with my crew on Wednesday to film the aesthetic changes."

"My head's spinning."

140

He cracked a smile. "It's a lot. I know. Normally, we'd have more time to work out these details, but it took us a while to find just the right store for our last episode."

"Why Rosie's Bridals?"

"Just a feeling." He touched her hand, igniting all the trepidation she'd managed to put aside while they poured through paperwork. "You'll see. This'll be great." He looked at his watch. "I'm going to head over to the nursing home to see my father and then head back to Hoboken. But first, let's have you sign the contract so I can deliver it to the producers in the morning. Where's the file?"

"Um, in my car, I think?" She couldn't remember where she'd put that folder. All she remembered was being asked to leave the conference room and going to the ladies' room to wash the cuff of her sweater where she'd sopped up a coffee spill. An old fear pricked her senses, and she cast him a side-glance. Here's where her scatterbrained tendencies would make the guy sorry he'd chosen her and her shop. She knew it would happen, but just not quite this soon.

"Okay, how about this? Let's go get it, and maybe you can drive me to The Memory Center up on Highland Avenue?"

"I can do that."

****

The file was not in her car. She checked under the seats, between them, and in the back. No file.

"I could have sworn it was in here." Rylee's face flushed despite the chill in the cold car. "I should have warned you that I tend to lose things. If you want to back out, I'd understand. Who could blame you?"

Was he annoyed? She couldn't tell. His face had a way of looking stern. The eyebrows were angled in on themselves, and his mouth was twisted to the side. *Yeah, he's pissed or looking for a way out or both.*

"Sorry, Darius."

He met her gaze, and his face softened. He was quite attractive when his face wasn't pinched. "We'll work it out. The problem, though, is that I'll have to get the contract into your hands tonight. I promised we'd have it on Jake's desk first thing in the morning. I technically shouldn't have gone over all your financials with you before that contract was signed. Can you meet me before eight in the morning? Unless you feel like driving to Hoboken tonight."

Her mind swirled. This was totally her fault. She remembered the way the lady looked when she'd managed to misplace her poodle. That dog-owner's face had had quite the pinch too.

"Let's go to Hoboken."

Chapter Twenty

Darius sat in the passenger seat as Rylee started the car. She pushed up the sun visor, adjusted her seat. Pulled some papers out of the cup holder and shoved them into a side pocket on the driver's side. She pulled off her gloves and shoved them into the cup holder, thought better of it, and stuffed them into her jacket pockets.

"Keys." Muttering, she withdrew a glove from one of the pockets. Shoved it back in. Did the other pocket the same way. Swore under her breath. "I just had them." She punched the button for the overhead light and looked around, between the seats, on the floor, in her purse twice. Finally, she withdrew the keychain from a zippered pouch of her purse. She uttered a chuckle. "Sorry."

Okay, it was going to be his job to chill her out. Filming would pick up any sign of her acting rattled or behaving like a veritable whack job, as Jake already suspected she was. He needed to dig deep for this. It was full steam ahead with the plan. Jake had texted him that Parker Paper was quote, unquote delighted about Rosie's Bridal shop for the episode. Jake had concerns about Rylee, thanks to that stupid video that college kid posted, and Darius could not, would not, prove him right.

She backed the car out of its parking place. She

chewed her lip. A tug twisted in his gut. There was something likable about this girl. She was quirky in a good way. He stifled a laugh for fear she'd think he was mocking her. She was obviously on edge about the misplaced file folder. Unless he could think of a way to distract her from her thoughts, the ride to his place would be tense. He could almost hear that brain of hers admonishing herself.

As they came to the light on Park and Main, he had an idea. "I have a deal for you. If you'll come with me to The Memory Center just to check in on my father, I'll treat for dinner at Jabberwocky's."

He could see her chest rise and fall despite the bulkiness of her down jacket.

"Ten minutes at the Center, tops. Just want to see the old guy for a minute. What do you say? It's just up the hill."

"I can do that." She chomped down on her lower lip again.

****

The Memory Center was a big old mansion on the other side of Sycamore River. Rylee remembered parking with boyfriends up on the outskirts of its grounds when she was a teenager. A couple of beer parties came to mind as well. Her gaze drifted over to Darius as they tread along the well-shoveled and salted walkway to the front doors.

"Thanks for doing this," he said.

She wanted to tell him she owed him. This mad scramble tonight was her fault, so yeah, he did not owe her any thank-yous. Instead, though, to not sound like too big a loser, she just nodded. She couldn't wait to tell Kit that the man, the pirate, whom she had sworn she'd manage to stay comfortably away from, was her copilot on this dark and freezing night. Nice one.

On the way down the quiet corridor, he turned to her. "He's got to leave this place soon."

"How come?"

"Money's running out."

She looked around at the artwork on the walls and the clean, clean everything. The lament in his voice pierced a pinprick in her heart. "So then what happens?"

Darius pulled a frown. "He's on a list for a state-run facility."

"Is it, you know, nice?"

"It's okay."

They reached his father's room. The bed closer to the door was empty, and his father sat on the end of his bed, facing the window. He fiddled with his pajama buttons. Maybe because he was old and frail looking, but as he turned when Darius called to him, she was surprised to see that he and Darius didn't look at all alike. This man was fair skinned, small and slight. His eyes were light, but rheumy and questioning. Not the sharp, compelling eyes of his son.

"Hey, Pop."

"Hello," the old man said.

"What are you doing there?" Darius went to him.

Rylee hung close to the edge of the other bed in the room and watched. She felt like an intruder in this intimate scene. She'd have a tough time forgetting the tender way Darius called his father "Pop."

"These buttons don't fit the holes." The old man gave the fabric a dismissive tug.

"Here, let's see." Darius crouched in front of his

father and worked on buttoning the pajama shirt.

The old man shooed him away. "Stop, boy. I can do this."

Darius looked up and met Rylee's gaze. A different kind of *zoom* tugged inside her, a brand-new kind. This had nothing to do with the sexiness that Darius Wirth's looks conjured. This was worse. If that damn poodle had looked at her with those eyes, she'd have never lost him.

"Pop, look. I brought a friend."

The old man twisted around and eyed her. She gave a little wave. "Hi, um, sir."

"Come here, girl. I can't see you."

She took two, then three steps to stand in front of the seated old man. He focused his foggy eyes on her, studied her face. "You're not Arabella."

Rylee looked up at Darius, and he gave her an encouraging look. "Pop, no. This is Rylee."

"Rylee? That's a boy's name, isn't it?"

"No." Darius chuckled. "If you can't see she's a girl, then you really do need new glasses."

She blushed. Something about his comment made her think he had catalogued that she was indeed female. The old powerful *zoom* flooded her bloodstream, only serving to add more heat to her face.

Darius's father squinted and craned his neck. "I'm pretty sure she's pretty." He looked around to Darius. "She your girlfriend?"

Darius chuckled. "Pop, she's going to let me film the renovations of her store for my show."

Pop screwed his countenance. Darius lost him with that one—Rylee could tell—and it was just as well because any more talk about whether she was Darius's girlfriend and she'd have a stroke with all the heat that flooded her face.

He successfully buttoned up his father and coaxed the old man to lie back on his pillow. He turned on the overhead television and found the right channel for the news. "Look, Pop. The remote is right next to your hand if you want to change channels."

"I'm tired."

"I know, Pop. Look, we're going to head out, let you rest, okay?"

"We? Is Arabella here?"

"No, look. Rylee's here with me. Remember?

The old man's face fell. "Okay."

****

On the way to Jabberwocky's, they were quiet. Rylee didn't know what to say, but questions ran through her head. Who was Arabella? Had Darius been married, or had this Arabella who was not her been a former love of his?

They ordered cheeseburgers—turned out they both liked jalapeño cheese. Darius had a beer, but because she was driving, she ordered a diet cola, which was such a ridiculous contrast to her big fat dinner.

"So that was my father," he said. "I wish you'd met the old guy before this disease robbed him of his personality. He was a heck of a guy. Funny too. Always teasing. Especially pretty girls."

Her face flushed again. "Who's Arabella?" She immediately regretted the question but couldn't pull it back.

"My mother. She died several years ago."

"Oh. I'm sorry."

He gave her an acknowledging nod. "Pop asks for

her all the time. He forgets she died. She was, uh, everything to him." He looked down at his plate and snatched a french fry. "Everything."

"That's so sweet," she said without thinking not to. "I always wished I'd had parents who were rock solid like that. You must have had a great childhood."

"It was good." He pinned her with his dark, shiny eyes. "Yours wasn't?"

"Not really." She coughed a little laugh, not out of humor but out of rawness. She felt raw and open and vulnerable, on a high dive blindfolded. "My growing up had a lot of drama. Father out in California finding himself, mother a marathon bride."

"Marathon bride?"

"Yeah. Including my father, she's on her fourth husband. But it's good. I like this one."

Darius laughed, and her mouth turned upward in response. "No, really. Sonny's a keeper."

"I'm sorry. I'm not laughing at the situation. You make me laugh."

"Yeah, I get that. I'm pretty laughable."

"No. That's not what I meant. What I mean is that your candidness is, let me think, refreshing."

"Refreshing."

"Yes."

She mulled it. She'd been called worse by much less attractive people. "I'll take it."

****

Rylee pulled her car into a parking space of his condominium complex on the water. The night was cold; the sky clear and bright with moonlight reflecting on leftover snow that had been plowed and piled up along the roadways and the perimeter of the lot. Darius, in his leather jacket, with the knot of woolen scarf at his neck and his black hair gleaming under the streetlamp, scared the bejesus out of her. Going into his apartment would normally be the straw that broke her resolve, but thankfully, there was a clause in that contract they were there to retrieve and sign. That clause insured that she would not *zoom* herself to stupidity royal. So for that, she breathed easier as they stood at his front door and he slipped his key into its lock. And just like that, she was wishing the pirate were a key and she a door lock.

Chapter Twenty-One

The apartment was spacious and urban sleek. Leather sofa, some chrome-and-glass tables, and shiny hardwood floors. The double set of sliding glass doors to the balcony were uncovered by curtains, and the Hudson River shimmered under the moonlight. It was a spectacular place.

"Can I get you something to drink?"

"I'm driving."

"How about a coffee? Unfortunately, I don't have caramel macchiato handy, but I do have a variety of coffee pods to pick from."

"Okay." *What harm in a cup of coffee?*

They sat on his couch, coffee mugs with steaming brew on the table in front of them. Darius pulled a copy of the contract out of a file he'd retrieved from some other room in the place. "Guess we're lucky I had my copy of the contract, huh? Saves us from having to hook up early in the morning before my meeting."

Yeah, so damn lucky to be here in this space alone with this man she could not touch. Lucky as hell.

While Darius perused the pages of the contract, she scanned the room. The fireplace surround was made of painted brick, the mantel a large hunk of wood that looked as if it were hacked off a tree yesterday. The mantel was bare, but on the brickwork above it was a large oil painting of a woman. She was beautiful, and the painting looked authentic, old, valuable.

"That's a great painting," she offered.

Darius glanced up from the paperwork. His mouth curved into a smile. "There's a story behind that painting."

"Oooo, I like stories."

"That's Arabella. Not my mother, but a rather famous artist's muse. Ever hear of Mabel Alvarez?"

"No, but that doesn't mean anything. I don't know much about art."

"Well, my mother was an avid art lover. Being Hispanic, she loved the works of several Spanish artists. Alvarez was her favorite, especially when she learned that the model's name was Arabella like her own."

"Wow, that's interesting."

"Yes, but that's not the whole story. When they were dating, my father was madly in love with my mother, and well, there was some Romeo and Juliet stuff that went on with their families. So my mother was hesitant to accept his marriage proposal. Turned him down once, but he asked again, but this time he presented her with the painting."

"Was it expensive?"

"For him back then it might as well have been a million dollars. But what it did cost him was his fishing boat."

"He sold his boat for the painting?"

"He did."

Rylee studied the painting, looking at it with new eyes. No matter how much is was worth in any art market, this was the most valuable painting she'd ever seen. It had cost a lot, and it had reaped quite a reward.

"That's just about the best story I've ever heard."

She held his gaze.

His mouth was a half smile, his eyes a pair of shiny stones. Rylee's chest constricted with the nearness of him, the scent of him, the allure of the man, pirate or no pirate. She swallowed a cinderblock.

"You, uh, need to sign this." He flipped to the last page of the contract. "Unless you need to go over the stipulations again."

"No, I don't need to go over it again."

"Okay, then."

"Okay, then."

He handed her a pen. With their gazes unflinching, he clicked the button at the end of the pen and the inky point poked out, ready. Ready to make this contract official, put all its stipulations in play.

She took the pen from his hand, and their fingers touched. Electricity charged through her veins. One sweep of her hand on the bottom line would lock her into this episode of a TV show, give Rosie's Bridals a better chance, a future for her store, her legacy. But, too, it would seal her into not touching this man on the sofa next to her, the man whose thigh was just inches from hers, whose eyes were on her. She eyed the pen, slipped her thumb up to the button, and felt the springy pressure of it on her skin. Heart racing, lungs immobile, she did what she had to do. She retracted the point and put the pen down on the coffee table.

"Not yet."

"I'm sorry?" His eyes held hers.

"I'm not ready for this contract to be signed."

Understanding showed bright in his eyes. His mouth opened, but he didn't speak. His chest lifted and fell in a deep breath. His Adam's apple dipped, rose.

"Neither am I," he said.

One tiny little move and Darius drew her into his arms. They were strong arms, and they held her tight. She felt delicate, feminine. His eyes asked if she was sure, and she responded the only way she knew how. She claimed his mouth in a bold kiss, enjoyed every millisecond of the *zoom* it sent through her system. She opened her mouth, welcomed him, and pressed closer.

A low groan sounded from deep within his throat, and their kiss intensified. He pulled her with him as he reclined onto the sofa, and before she knew it, she was on top of him, her chest crushed to his chest, her hips calling to his. There was no contract, no show to worry about, no inherited store to think about. There was just this. This man, this pirate who was proof positive she was not nuts and there was chemistry between two people that was purely organic. Later, she'd worry about what would happen beyond this moment. She didn't care. She wouldn't think. She would only feel.

Darius squeezed a hand between their pressed bodies and fumbled with the button to her jeans. She broke their kiss, and in the lamplight of his living room, she pinned his gaze. Were they doing this? *Yeah. Yup. Yessiree.*

Rylee pushed herself up, her legs straddling him. His hands nimbly undid the metal button of her Levi's and drew the zipper pull down slowly as the teeth opened, welcomed, revealed the patch of fabric of her panties. Blue with white polka dots and an appliqué of a slice of watermelon. When she'd purchased the packet of five panties at the discount department store, little had she known they'd be seen and even fondled by the most appealing man she'd ever laid eyes on.

Darius ran the pad of his thumb over the appliqué of the watermelon slice at her hip. His thumb moved back and forth and then trailed downward. His thumb pad circled round and round, massaging the fabric. She thumped low inside, and her hips responded to the movement by a slow roll, round and round like a dance. She arched her back, tilted her pelvis forward, and continued the slow roll of her hips. Finally, Darius moaned again and sat up, gripped her hips with his mighty hands, and peeled her garments away.

In a flurry of greedy hands, their clothes were off and covering the cushiony carpet in a haphazard pile. With mouths locked, breaths rapid, their kiss was hungry, raw, and relentless. His hands travelled over her eager skin, pausing to massage, knead, caress. She kissed his neck, bit into the flesh of his shoulder. She breathed him in, burrowed into the patch of hair of his chest.

With unrelenting need, Rylee allowed herself to take and be taken. He slipped inside her, the fit complete, satisfying, perfect. Her hands gripped the taut mound of his bottom, and she wrapped her legs around him as they moved together, slow and then fast, deliciously maddening. As he bucked in release, her fingernails dug into his flesh as her own dizzying pulsations overtook her. She wouldn't allow any thoughts to crack into the liquid bliss of this moment. No. Tonight was for this, and that was all that mattered.

Chapter Twenty-Two

Rylee stood in front of the mirror in Darius's sleek black-and-white-tiled bathroom. Her hair was a crazy whirl that stuck out from her face, and she looked a bit clownish with her mascara coloring the skin under her eyes with black half moons. Her eyes, though, were what compelled her, and she could not look away. *What did you do?* The eyes taunted her. *What the hell did you do now, Einstein?*

Fully-dressed and her face washed, she opened the door to the bathroom and slowly walked down the hallway to the living room. Darius was there in his jeans, no socks or shoes, his shirt unbuttoned. He had placed two new cups of coffee on the table and a bag of Oreos. He lifted the package when she came into the room and gave it a little wag.

"Hungry?" His grin was shameless.

"Uh, it's getting kind of late."

He dropped the bag onto the coffee table and pointed to the steaming cups of coffee. "Come here, Rylee. Have some coffee."

Inside her head the taunts continued. *Now what are you going to do, smart aleck?* How was she supposed to be around this specimen of manhood and not think about what they just did? She swallowed hard and stepped closer to him, careful not to touch, and accepted the coffee cup he extended her way. "Thank

155

you," she muttered, avoiding his eyes.

He sat on the couch and patted the cushion next to him. "Have a seat."

She didn't move.

"Come on. Sit."

She was reminded again of the poodle she'd managed to lose in the woods. That damn dog didn't listen for shit, and that sucked. So, like a good poodle and against her better judgment, she sat next to Darius. Yet she continued to avoid his gaze.

"Rylee." The way he said her name was as if he were the parent and she were the toddler who had just written on the dining room wall with her crayons, a practice she'd enjoyed back then but had outgrown years ago. "Are you regretting this?"

"Are you?"

He blew out a lungful of air. A hand raked through his jet-black hair, which she knew now was softer than it looked. His dark gaze implored her.

Inside she *zoomed* as she'd never *zoomed* before. Her insides took the ride, up, down, and again, an elevator on crack.

"What I regret, dear girl, is that we can't do that again."

"Ha-ha. Well, I think we just complicated everything."

"Tell me how."

"For one thing, we have to be in each other's company day in and day out, and we are going to be expected to act all professional and everything. I don't know about you, but I'm not much of an actor. I can't be responsible for behaving like this." She waved her hands back and forth between them. "This *stuff* didn't happen."

"Look," he said. "I like you. Obviously." He uttered a laugh, and just like that, her mind's eye gave her an up-close-and-personal glimpse of what they must have looked like rolling around like baby pandas in this very room just minutes ago. *Somebody, stab me.*

"You're not helping."

He chuckled and shook his head.

"Please don't laugh. I'm wondering if your balcony is high enough for me to effectively leap right off it to end my misery."

"Okay, come on. Granted, the timing of our meeting is personally less than ideal, but think about what is *ideal* regarding our meeting. I'm going to help you keep your grandmother's bridal shop up and running, give a whole new life to the place. And you're helping me keep my TV show on the air. It's perfect."

Perfect? Was that what this pirate was all about? Were one-night stands his norm? Well, she passed the couch test. That was one consolation. She couldn't logically be mad at the guy because, in truth, she was the one who kissed him first and what followed had been all okay, more than okay, the freaking halleluiah of all okays. So all she had was herself to blame. As freaking usual.

"I'm going to go."

"Um, we still need your signature." Darius reached for the pen and the pages of the contract.

"Of course." Rylee took the pen and scribbled her name, unable to see through a sudden blurring of unbidden tears. Crying was uncalled for. It wasn't as if she hadn't known that this was a one-time roll in the hay. Why, though, did she feel so lousy? Sad. She felt sad. It was like suddenly finding just what you were looking for and realizing the prize wasn't meant for you. She blinked away the tears.

His hand moved to her arm, fingers warm on her skin. *And why would you think touching me would make things better? Do not put your skin on my skin anymore.*

"We should have thought this through, huh?"

She met his gaze and twisted her mouth into a sideways bunch. "Yup."

"Oh boy, I'm—"

"Don't." She didn't want him to say he was sorry. *Don't be sorry.* As much as it sucked that tonight was a one-time memory, she couldn't look at it as something to apologize for. She suspected that when she was eighty years old and rocking in her rocking chair, hopefully still drinking vodka, she would remember this night. But, God help her, she couldn't tell Darius that.

"Tell me how I can help make this easier."

She blew out a long breath. *What the hell.* "Open the Oreos."

Chapter Twenty-Three

A hand shoved aside the curtain to one of the dressing cubicles, the rings moving across the aluminum rod with an annoying metal-on-metal screech. On her knees Rylee looked up from her task of painting the baseboard. A zip of annoyance shot through her. The camera guys had only been in the shop for a couple of hours, and already she wanted them gone. Technically, she wanted the whole deal gone, behind her. Over. And the fact that Darius was treating her as if she had a bad case of leprosy—well, that was just ducky.

But the person standing behind her was not a cameraman or anybody else from *Wirth More*. The whole crew had taken a lunch break and had gone out for sandwiches. This was Kit filling up the space with her eyes wide and just short of googly. Kit was into the whole let's-be-on-TV thing, and her gung-ho attitude only served to feed Rylee's ire.

Kit tugged the curtain closed behind her and pressed her knuckles to her hips.

"What?" Rylee stood from her kneeling position, paintbrush still in hand.

"What the hell is wrong with you?" Kit's voice was a whispered rasp.

"You don't have to whisper. They're out for lunch."

"I don't understand what's up with you."

"Nothing," she shot, hotter than she'd intended. "I'm doing my job. I was told to paint the baseboard molding, so I'm painting the baseboard molding."

"You're acting, I don't know, mad. Are you mad?"

Rylee blew out a puff of air. "No."

"What, then?"

"Maybe I'm not all yay about this TV crap like you are. That's all. I'm doing what I have to do." She saluted her paintbrush. "See?"

"These people are here to help us, Ry. Lighten up."

"Oh, you mean like you and that giggling you've been doing? Since when do you giggle?"

"I don't."

Rylee harrumphed. "Wait till they play back the footage, friend. You'll see. You sound like a twelve-year-old invited to her first boy-girl party."

Kit shrugged. "That pirate of yours is pretty funny. He seems really nice too."

Rylee opened her mouth to speak, then snapped her jaw closed. "I need to finish painting."

"It's about him, isn't it? Oh my God, Rylee. I get it. You don't hate these people. You're crushing on the pirate."

She let the paintbrush fall to the drop cloth and grabbed Kit by the upper arms. "Will you please keep your voice down? They could have sneaked back in."

They stared at each other for a long moment and, finally, Kit spoke. "It's no crime to like the guy, Rylee."

"Yes, it is," she said to Kit's screwed-up face. "Remember there's a contract in place that says no fraternizing whatsoever or we lose the money and

Darius loses his job. So, yeah, it's a crime."

"Wow. Okay. You know what, though? I'm thinking about his behavior now. Is this why he's been interacting with everybody but you?"

A flush of heat climbed up her cheeks, and her mouth went dry. Her swallow was sandpaper. She couldn't look away from Kit's inquiring stare.

"Did something happen between you two?"

"Kit..."

Kit sucked in her breath. "You didn't, you know, screw him or anything, did you?"

Rylee sighed aloud. "To. The. Wall."

"Hey," a voice called. It was one of the crew. It sounded like Donald, the short guy with the Santa Clause beard. "We're back. Anybody here?"

"Yes," Rylee called out. "Kit and I are here painting." She bent down and gripped the paintbrush. She jabbed it toward her best friend. "And don't try lecturing me, dammit."

"Lecture you," Kit scoffed. "I'm dying for details."

"Nope. Not saying anything."

"Well, at least tell me one thing. Was it worth it? I mean, did you feel that elusive *zoom* you talk so much about?"

Rylee looked up at the ceiling. "I'm still *zooming.*"

"Who's *zooming?*" The curtain to the dressing cubicle opened, and there stood another one of the camera guys, the one named Jimmy with glasses, a salt-and-pepper goatee, and an easy smile. "Paint fumes getting to you, ladies?"

"Ha." She feigned a laugh. "I guess so."

"Well, you've got to keep that curtain open, darlin'. Okay, the boss wants us to take some more footage of you at work. You ready for this?"

"Sure." She stole a glance at her friend. "Ready."

****

It was still alive in Darius. Technically, the experience with Rylee hadn't broken any of the network's rules. The paperwork hadn't been signed yet when they had decided to get busy. But the fact that the ink was on the line now and that it meant hands off for a period not less than three years bothered him more than was comfortable. The night had been hot, good and hot, but what rolled around his mind and travelled down to his chest was the look on her face as they sat together on his sofa, silence between them except for the sound of the cellophane bag of cookies that their hands intermittently reached into. Among the crunching sounds, the heaviness of *never again* hung in the air like a bow of pine laden with snow.

He remembered the way dark chocolate cookie crumb clung to her lip, the way her teeth scraped the white icing off the dark disk of the cookie and her tongue closed over it. Her pretty mouth working to devour the confection just about did him in. A smile threatened his lips at the memory of Rylee jutting her hand up to him without pulling her eyes from her task of eating an Oreo. Her accusation, "I can see you watching me," and the order, "Keep your eyes to yourself." The best, though, had been her "I really only came here for the cookies."

Rylee MacDermott was a paradox. She hadn't once acted as if he alone had been responsible for their ill-timed romp. She even managed to laugh as they ate cookies on the couch, did her best to muster some levity. But now in the light of day with his crew here in her store and Rylee's employees flitting about, all he could think of was wanting to kiss her, to suck that soft lower lip of hers into his mouth and claim it.

"Darius, you got a minute?" Jake stood in front of him, knuckles pressed to his hips.

"What's up?"

"Can you talk to this chick? Liven her up a little or something?"

"Is Rylee too stiff?"

"Not if we were shooting a drywall commercial. But she's not showing us anything that we need. I know just what the big guns are going to say when they see what we've shot. They're going to ask how the audience is supposed to feel her need for our show to rescue her. There's no fire in this person, Darius."

Wanna bet? Darius forced his mind away from just how much fire that woman could produce. "Okay. I'll talk to her."

"But I wanted to tell you that the idea for the fashion show was brilliant."

"Really? Good."

"Yeah, and I've got the perfect plan for the happy-ending bit."

The thought of pulling a fast one on Rylee gave his insides a wringing. "What have you got in mind?"

"We're going to have the gowns neglect to arrive."

"No." Venom shot through Darius's veins.

"What do you mean no. Thanks to you, my friend, the dresses are going to show up just in the nick of time." Jake jabbed his shoulder with his fist. "*Wirth More*'s own superhero."

"I just don't think that's necessary. I mean, the show's going to be good without having to pull that stunt."

Jake shrugged. "You want a second season, don't you?"

Darius could not tamp down the thought of his father moving from the warm cocoon of The Memory Center all because his only son couldn't get his act together.

"Yeah. "

"So full steam ahead, then. Now go talk to her and loosen her up."

He managed to catch her eye, something he'd avoided all day, and they were beacons of warning, an opposite traffic light. When it came to Rylee's eyes today, the compelling green meant stop.

"Can we talk for a second?" He motioned toward the stockroom and proceeded as though she had already agreed.

****

Rylee took a deep breath and entered the stockroom. Darius in his crisp chambray shirt, cuffs rolled up to the elbow, big fat silver watchband on his dark wrist, made keeping her eyes from feasting nearly impossible. She tried blinking away his appeal and felt like a human Morse code machine.

"Hi." His mouth was a slant.

"Hi."

"You doing okay?"

"Sure. Fine. Why?"

"Rylee, come sit." He motioned to one of the metal stools at the worktable.

She came closer but did not sit. She saw the way his black jeans stretched over his thighs, spread, as he straddled one of the stools. *Oh God.* She blinked an

SOS. "Is there a problem?" Besides the fact that she wanted to sit on his lap and take that metal stool for a spin?

"The guys wanted to know if we can, um, work on your being more animated."

"Animated."

"You know, more engaging, more into it."

"I warned you going in, Darius, that I'm no actor."

"Sure, that's fine. But you think you can muster some enthusiasm? You know, act like you're up about the shop's renovation and what that can mean for your business. Be in it, so to speak."

They held a long glance. She wanted to "be in it," and she didn't want to act like a snot. But this was tough. Having this man in front of her turned her insides into a carnival ride.

When he reached what she could not forget was a strong-yet-gentle hand across to her, she pulled away as if he were shooting lighter fluid. "Don't," she whispered.

"I'm sorry."

"Stop. I told you there's nothing to be sorry about." She drew in a lungful of air and let it expel.

"There's a lot riding on this episode, as you know. The success of your store and my job's future."

A swath of heat climbed up her face. Flashes of Darius' dilemma darted through her mind, the way he looked at his little frail father curled up in a bed at the nursing home. And that painting in his apartment, the woman who resembled his mother, the pride in his eyes when he'd told the story. Her insides sunk. She needed to get over herself for both their sakes. "I'll do better tomorrow."

"If it helps at all, the guys say the camera loves you."

She zeroed in on the way a smile played over his lips, a rueful turn of his mouth that tugged deep in her chest. He might be wishing things were different too, and that made it all the worse.

"I was worried that on camera I might look like a tank, you know, due to what I've come to call "the Oreo incident.""

Now he laughed and shook his head. "Not a chance."

She managed to rivet her eyes away from him and turned on her heel. She marched out of the stockroom, determined to look forward and get through these next few days come hell or high water.

"By the way, Rylee…"

She turned back to him. "Yeah?"

"Just a heads-up. Tomorrow they're spending most of the day shooting the two of us interacting." His shiny eyes bore onto hers, assessing and black like ink. "It's called the 'One on One' segment."

"That's not a problem." *As long as I can find a drive-through lobotomy center.*

"Good."

"Good." *Shoot me.*

Chapter Twenty-Four

Somehow, Rylee didn't know how, she managed to sit next to the pirate, to inhale the scent of his manliness, to feel his man heat, and go over paperwork while on camera. Because her brain was rice pudding, it helped that the major stuff of the details had already been established and this shuffle of paper was primarily for the show's sake.

She was nervous during her phone call to the bridal house that would be shipping the sample order to her store for the fashion show. The house assured her that the sample gowns would arrive next Thursday, two full days before Saturday's fashion show, which gave her time to learn the details of each dress so she could give a commentary as the models paraded them. The cram session would be a study in the difference between chiffon and georgette and whatever the hell shantung was. And necklines, God help her.

These brides-to-be were savvy. They knew what a semisweetheart neckline was as compared to a full-blown sweetheart. She wouldn't be able to fool them. She needed to remember things like a bateau style was a boat neckline. And she'd have to let those terms roll off her tongue as if she were fluent in the vernacular. How she was going to speak in front of a roomful of soon-to-be brides and their entourages was beyond her. Darius and *Wirth More* had arranged for three models for the fashion show, and Kit would be assisted by Linda and Freda in organizing the dressing and undressing. They kept talking about it being all in the timing. She majorly sucked at timing, the testament being the man who started this whole mess.

They went over the flyers they planned to distribute to the other stores in town. The show had bought radio time on the local station as well as a TV spot on their cable network. An online media blast had gone out and was getting lots of hits. God only knew how many people would show up for this shindig. Her knees were knocking already.

"We covered a lot of territory today, Rylee." Darius grinned. "We're going to be ready for Saturday's fashion show."

She didn't like this smile he produced for the cameras. It wasn't him. Somehow she knew that. "I hope so."

And with that, the cameras were off and the taping session was done. The cameramen and the light guys went off to the far side of the room to load up their equipment, which left Darius and Rylee alone at the desk.

She blew out a breath. "How do you do this all the time?"

"You get used to it. It becomes like second nature."

"Huh."

"What's that mean?"

"It's nothing."

"No, Rylee, what did you mean by that?"

"Your smile." She pointed a hesitant finger at his mouth. "You have a different one for the camera."

"Do I?" His mouth cut into a genuine curve.

"Really?"

She nodded.

"No one's ever said that to me before." His head tilted in contemplation.

"Well, trust me. You do." She turned to face him fully. "When the cameras are on, you do this." She pulled what felt like a clownish grin.

Darius laughed out loud. "I do not."

"Yes, you do." She did the clown mouth again.

"Stop it."

She couldn't help the bubble of laughter that escaped her lips. "Kind of Ronald McDonaldish."

"Okay, now you're making it up."

"I'm not kidding. And trust me. I know a little something about that mouth of yours."

And like that, they froze. Darius turned his attention to the crew members who busily zipped equipment into carriers. He pulled his gaze back to Rylee.

Sorry, she mouthed.

"They didn't hear anything," he uttered, his voice low. "Don't worry." He touched her arm.

She looked down at his hand on her sleeve and was reminded of the night at his apartment. "I don't think you should be touching me, Ronald McDonald."

He smiled a real smile.

"See that." She pointed at his mouth. "Now that's a real one."

"You make me smile." He squeezed her arm, and even though it was on top of the fabric of her shirtsleeve, her skin began to tingle. "And I wish…"

"Don't." Her insides squeezed. "Please."

He let his hand fall away, and the smile went with

it.

****

When the day was done, Rylee turned down Kit's invitation to join her and the girls for drinks and burgers at Jabberwocky's. She just couldn't face any questions about Darius now that she'd been fool enough to let Kit know the two of them had had sex. Just that word threatened to conjure the memory of his body entwined with hers, the intensity of it all.

Climbing up to her apartment, she fought against the images playing in her head. She wanted to put on her sweats and pour herself a glass of merlot and shut off her mind.

A while later after a gourmet dinner of peanut butter on a day-old bagel, she sat on the living room sofa, sinking into the overstuffed softness of the cushions. She sipped the pungent red wine she poured for herself and closed her eyes. But all she could see in her imagination was Darius. His swashbuckler's smile, the face she'd come to decide was quite handsome, his masculine appeal palpable. She groaned aloud, and the sound echoed in the stillness of the space.

She put the glass down on the coffee table and zeroed in on Rosie's photo album of thank-you notes and photos from happy brides. She flipped open the cover, a welcome distraction from her thoughts. She'd make a game out of guessing the details of the dresses.

A young bride with her groom, glamorous in their wedding-day finery, she in a sateen—was it sateen?—square-neck A-line, stared out from a photograph, grins wide. She remembered the bride, Shelby Britton. Shelby had been the bride with the weight problem, who cried when she saw herself in the mirror wearing the gown Rosie had helped her select. Somehow they'd chosen a gown that had turned a woman self-conscious of her size into a regal princess. Rylee took a sip of her merlot as she eyed Shelby's beaming smile. It said confidence, happiness, love.

The accompanying note was gushy, and Rylee smiled despite the fact that she herself was not a gushy type.

She turned the page. Megan Harris. A dark-haired beauty with all the money to import herself a gown from any designer in Europe. But nope. She'd fallen in love with the little town of Sycamore River when she'd come to town for a college friend's wedding. She'd met and eventually became engaged to a local guy and decided on a quaint wedding at the Episcopalian chapel on the green. The photo of Megan in a liquid satin sheath and her groom was a stunner, and Rylee's heart hurt seeing their obvious love and knowing the young bride's husband had been killed in a car wreck last year. She touched her finger to the photo encased in plastic. She wondered how Megan was now.

Rylee went page by page. Some brides she knew; some she did not. Some gowns she could name; some she could not. Everyone, though, had a story of love and gratitude. All the thank-you notes had praised Rosie's attention to their needs and wants, the shop's going over and above for them, that personal touch attributable to Rosie. Granted, the whole crew at Rosie's was mentioned from time to time—even Rylee herself, shock of all shocks—but the main theme was the charisma and acumen of Rosie.

She closed the album and finished her wine. How on earth was she supposed to follow in those footsteps?

How the hell was she going to make people still want Rosie's Bridals as their wedding expert when the expert was dead?

Chapter Twenty-Five

On the last day of shooting, Rylee was a roller coaster of feelings—glad she wouldn't have to be in Darius's constant company and yet bummed, too, that it was soon over. A whole week would pass before she'd see him again at the final shoot for the fashion show.

She'd be busy in the coming days. Brides-to-be were booked for the event, and the promo had only just gone out. Most brides were bringing their mothers along. The companionship made sense, but the mother-daughter duos made Rylee think about the few times in her life, particularly during high school, when she'd allowed herself to imagine her own future wedding. Always the scenario had been her and Rosie fawning over a dress. It saddened her that her mother was never in the imagined prospect. Sad for one mother figure who was gone and the other one here yet beyond reach.

Darius and the crew arrived, and her heart did its dance when he looked at her. She was just a nuclear reactor when it came to the guy. Maybe, with any luck at all, the chemical reaction to Darius Wirth would go away when he did.

They filmed the setting up of chairs and a portable runway. Rylee and the girls fit tulle bows around the chairbacks and hot-glued silk tea roses at each knot. In truth, Rylee's bows had to be redone, and she somehow glued fabric roses to her hair. Although she had hoped that part of the filming could be cut from the final edits, the guys told her no way. They'd said her foibles made for better TV. If that was the case, then maybe she had a future as a TV star.

They completed the work by four in the afternoon. A round of applause sounded among the crew and Rylee's coworkers while she, nervously picking dried glue from her fingertips, stood at the opposite end of the room and did her best to avoid the shiny black gaze of Darius Wirth.

What would life be like to never see him again after all this? *Never again.* It sucked. But in one way she wouldn't change what had happened between them. She wadded up the tissue she'd used to catch the flecks of dried glue she'd scraped from her fingers, and she tossed it in the trash. She felt his gaze even before she lifted her head. He watched her. Meeting his gaze, holding it for a long moment, she knew in that instant she was grateful for one thing. She knew it now, that chemistry between two people, that seductive *zoom.* Darius Wirth would be a tough act to follow.

Jake, the boss from the show, arrived at the store. He was a nice-looking man as well. Tall and straight, with confidence in his walk and a direct look in his eyes. No-nonsense kind of guy. His smile, though, didn't reach his eyes. He had no laugh lines by his eyes as Darius did, nor was there ever a flash of amusement in his gaze. Not that it did her one bit of good to compare him or anyone to Darius.

After Jake greeted Darius, the two of them came up to her. Jake reached out to shake her hand, and she was grateful her fingers were now glue free.

"How did it go, Rylee?" His mouth pulled into that

pretend smile, kind of an elastic snap.

"Okay, I guess."

"Excited for the fashion show next week?"

"Nervous too."

"Ah, don't be," Jake said. He slapped a hand to Darius's shoulder. "This guy will make sure it runs smooth. Right, buddy?"

"Absolutely." Darius's mouth slid into an easy smile.

She liked those easy smiles. He had such a good mouth. *Lordy.*

Before she knew it, everyone was discussing going to Jabberwocky's downtown for drinks and a bite. Socializing with the *Wirth More* gang and her workers was the last thing she wanted to do, but Kit wasn't having excuses.

"You have to come," she said in a hot whisper. "It's your store."

Rylee smiled through gritted teeth. "I need to spend more time with that man like I need a hole in my head."

Darius and Jake stood nearby, and she could tell by the way Darius's eyebrows tilted in on themselves that he either heard their exchange or surmised she was dragging her feet on going off to party with everyone.

"Hey, listen. You guys go on ahead to Jabberwocky's. I need to go check on my father."

His eyes were on Rylee, and she knew without needing the words that besides wanting to see his dad, he was exiting the scene for her sake, a confirmation that this was serious. Nobody, especially not Jake, could suspect anything had happened between the two of them. Yeah, it would be an embarrassment if the show pulled its funding for all the things they'd provided to Rosie's Bridals. She knew how to grapple with embarrassment. Hell, she lost a poodle, for God's sake. But she could not live with herself if Darius lost his job.

"We'll save you a seat," Jake said. "My best to your father."

Darius cast his gaze over to her, and the message in it said goodbye.

****

On his way out the door, Darius felt a hand on his arm. For a millisecond he thought it might be Rylee telling him to stay, to join them at Jabberwocky's. But that was crazy. The girl was off limits. She knew it. He knew it. It was Jake.

"Hold up," Jake said in a low tone. His eyes skittered across the workers gathering their things, slipping into their coats, readying to make the trek to the restaurant. "I want to talk with you a second." His face was stern, his mouth a seam on his face.

What was his problem now? This was what the guy did all the time. A perfectionist, he looked for trouble. With their show's renewal on the line, Darius couldn't blame him, though. So he pinned on a smile. "Sure. What's up?"

"You and the screwball chick."

"Stop calling her that. What about her?"

"You're not messing around with her, are you?"

"What?" Darius's insides turned over on themselves. "Are you crazy?"

Jake grabbed his phone and swiped at the screen. With a determined jerk of his finger, he connected to a social media site and faced the device to Darius. "Can you explain this, then?"

He stared at the random photo of himself and Rylee from when they were at Jabberwocky's. In the picture they leaned in close to each other, which in all fairness was due to the bar's din. But their coziness looked as if they were really into each other.

"This is nothing, man. She had given me a ride up to see my father, and I offered to buy her a burger. You know how this goes, Jake. Somebody recognized me from the show and posted the picture. End of story."

"No. Not the end of the story. Read the comments."

"No, thanks."

"Okay, well, let's just say people are wondering about you and this woman."

Darius pulled a face. "Just let it go. It'll go away."

"I've just got this vibe, man. There's a high price for jeopardizing our show. I know you know that. And it's not me so much I worry about if we're all out of work." He swept his hand wide. "It's these guys."

Yeah, right.

"I'm aware." Darius swallowed hard. Technically, he wasn't lying. His and Rylee's moment had been before the papers were signed. Everything about this, though, felt like crap. Because in truth their time together was more than that one night in his apartment. A connectedness existed, some tie to her. She was all he thought about. Even trying not to think about her was futile. And he loved her quirkiness. He forced himself not to look across the room to where she was. Especially not with Jake staring him down.

"Just making sure," Jake said. "Parker Paper gets any inclination that you're too cozy with her and they're out. I've gone over most of the promo pictures the guys took, and I swear there are some shots with you and her that look like—"

"For God's sake, Jake. Stop." Darius's heart stalled in his chest.

But he proceeded. "Like you two are banging. That's what it looked like. And if I think it, then maybe the fans watching the promo spots might think it too. And then the sponsor gets antsy. Get me?"

"You're talking nonsense, Jake. But, yes, I get you."

"You need something to focus on? Start thinking about the new season. And let somebody else handle any wacko women that cross your path."

"Stop."

"Stop what?

There was no sense in arguing. Rylee wasn't any wacko or screwball. Yeah, she was unique in her demeanor, a little self-deprecating, and she had a quirkiness that he'd come to think was endearing. But no way was he going to tell Jake any of that.

"Darius, you joining us after all." Jimmy bundled into his down coat and New Jersey Devils hat.

"Sorry, no," Darius said, being sure to keep his eyes from finding Rylee. "Going to see my old man for a bit."

Jake punched Darius's shoulder. "Make sure you stop by. I want to take a photo with everyone for social media. You need to be part of that—front and center, actually. Okay?"

"Okay."

"Don't be too long."

****

Darius watched his father sleep, his dinner

untouched on its tray. The coagulating gloppy food was nothing short of disgusting. How did anybody eat this shit? His father couldn't have solid foods until, or if, he passed what they called a "swallow test." So unless that happened, he'd be given this putrid-smelling mound of gray matter on a dish. Darius's stomach pitched.

His father stirred, grumbled, and sucked in a loud breath. His eyes flittered open, and he tried to focus his gaze. His gray-blue eyes had been so sharp, so assessing, so telling, back when he had a quick mind working its wheels behind them. Now they were flat disks.

"You're awake," Darius said.

His father's mouth pulled down into an exaggerated frown. "Get this crap out of here." He gave his table a shove, and the tray slid sideways and tipped over the edge, spilling the gunk all over the floor with gooey spots dotting the bed sheets and one of Darius's pant legs.

"Oh shit." Darius jumped up from the chair. He grabbed at a stack of paper towels and blotted his messed jeans. "Jesus."

"Don't just stand there," his father barked. "Clean this up."

"Let me get somebody." He went to the door and peered down the hallway, looking for an orderly or somebody. "Hey, can we get a hand in here?" he shouted to a tall guy pushing a mop bucket.

The guy came into the room and assessed the damage, assured him they'd get his father cleaned up "in a jiffy" and asked through the intercom for a nurse's aide to come in to help Pop change. The aide, a middle-aged woman named Sadie, popped in with an armload of linens. A grin claimed her lipsticked mouth.

"What happened, Mitch?" she said with a hint of whimsy, as if Pop were a rambunctious yet adorable puppy with a bedroom slipper caught in his teeth. The mop guy whistled, as if instead of performing his disgusting task, he were picking daisies. What kind of people were these? Where did one find folks like this, and did they exist in state-run facilities? The chance that his father would not be taken as good care of as he was now at The Memory Center made him feel worse. He didn't want to fail this old man.

He looked at the old guy as the kind hands of The Memory Center employees cleaned him. When they were through, the woman, Sadie, ran a soft hand over the crown of Pop's head. "All better now," she cooed. "You feel better now, Mitch?"

Somehow he needed to keep his father right where he was.

"Are you hungry, Pop?"

The old man tried to focus his gaze. "Who are you?"

"Pop, it's me. Darius."

"Oh." His mouth curled into a craggy, garish grin. "Hi, son. Didn't see you there."

Pop did not remember lashing out at him—the harshness of his behavior was just another aspect of his disease. Mitch Wirth had been a tough but good guy before this bastard Alzheimer's had come calling. But the agitated episode was over for now.

"You remember your dinner tray fell? Want me to get you something to eat?"

"I don't care." His father yawned. "Where's your mother?"

There was no use in going through the conversation again. It would only serve to upset his father. Instead he said, "I'll be right back." He left the room in search of someone who could get him a can of that sick-smelling protein drink his father managed to ingest and keep down.

He came back with the can, a straw jabbed into the open top. "Look, I brought you a milkshake."

His father accepted the can into his feeble grasp. He took a sip. "Where's your lady friend?"

"How's that?"

"You know, that girl you brought with you yesterday."

Rylee had been with him for a visit several days ago, not yesterday. He was surprised, though, that his father even remembered her, but that was another thing about the disease. Short-term memory still had a chance of surfacing.

"You mean Rylee?"

"Yeah, the pretty girl with the boy name."

Darius smiled. His father could always tell a pretty lady. His mother would tease him about it, call him a shameless flirt if he'd been caught charming a waitress for an extra dollop of ice cream on his apple pie or some such favor.

"Yes, that's her." Darius consulted his watch. It was getting near time for him to head over to the restaurant and join the others. First, though, he'd need to go to the men's room and clean his pant leg with some soap and water. "I have to leave pretty soon, Pop. I'm going to go see her, as a matter of fact."

"Is your mother gone?" The old man put the drink onto his tray and rested his head against his pillows.

"She died, didn't she? I've lost her."

Darius's chest locked. He couldn't avoid this now. "Yes."

Quick tears flooded his rheumy eyes. That was another thing. Mitch had never been the type to cry, never prone to tears. But this was now.

He went over to his father and laid a hand on his shoulder. He was skinny, his bones sharp under thin skin.

"You know something, though, Pop. She's still in your heart, right?"

"Who is?"

Now tears sprang into his own eyes. The moment was over. Pop was back into his fog, and what hurt right now was that it was a relief. Reliving the pain of losing his beloved Arabella over and over was just too much.

He patted his father. "I'm going to head out, Pop. I'll see you soon, okay?"

But his father had already closed his eyes, and the rhythmic sound of his mucusy intake and exhale of breath told him Pop was already asleep. Darius pulled the can of protein drink from his loose grasp and placed it on his father's table.

****

The *Wirth More* people and the sponsors from the paper company were buying drinks all around, and Rylee was on her second champagne cocktail. While she nibbled on a triangle of chicken quesadilla, she strained to listen to the conversation going on around her. The energy was high among the show's crew, and the guys in suits from Parker Paper were all puffed up with their self-imposed importance.

Everyone was abuzz about the upcoming fashion show, and the paper execs thought that it would be a fine way to end the show's season. The people from *Wirth More* beamed at their words, but Jake was kind of quiet. It seemed odd. He was one of those guys who liked to be out there, high-fiving all over the place and acting all proud, as if he'd singlehandedly pulled this all off. But tonight he and his drink of some dark liquid on the rocks just watched, his steady gaze zeroed in on her.

What was his problem? Rylee sipped her drink. She had other things to worry about. Like wrestling with a duality of wishes. She hoped Darius would skip this event entirely so she wouldn't have to see him and be near him and pretend she wasn't into him. The stronger wish whipped around inside her with zooming velocity—wanting him to arrive. She downed the rest of her drink in time for a waiter to deliver her a third.

Before she could take a single sip of the new champagne cocktail, the door to Jabberwocky's opened, and God help her, the pirate filled the room with his presence.

****

He kept his distance from Rylee yet was troubled that she may feel slighted by his obvious lack of attention. Jake's eyeballs were on him, and Darius didn't like the smirk on the guy's face. He ordered himself a Jameson and joined in a conversation with his coworkers. All the while, though, he sensed Jake's penetrating gaze.

"Hey, Darius," one of the guys from Parker Paper called from where he sat at the bar. "Join us."

He made his way over to the sponsor reps and did his best to ignore the brunette across the room. But the more days that went by, the more he found himself thinking about her, wondering about her.

A couple of women at the bar eyeballed the crowd, craning their necks to try to listen. Darius wondered if they recognized him from the show, but their attention seemed to be directed toward Rylee. Maybe one of them was a would-be bride interested in the upcoming fashion show, and if that was the case, he hoped they'd approach her. It would be great for Parker's folks to see that the locals were responding to their ads. The women made their way over to Rylee, and he slid his eyes to Jake to make sure he was paying attention. This would keep the guy happy.

Chapter Twenty-Six

"Excuse me." A tall redhead with glasses tapped her on the shoulder. "We just wanted to say hi and tell you how inspiring you are."

Rylee put down her empty drink glass. *What? Inspiring?* "I'm not sure what you mean." She looked around to see that Kit and the other girls from her shop had stopped talking and were listening in.

The woman accompanying the redhead, a black girl with a bright-eyed look and killer lashes, held a hand to her chest. "You have no idea how many women's lives you're touching."

Now she laughed. Maybe it was the champagne sloshing around in her stomach, but the idea that these people were telling *her* that *she* was an inspiration was just that—laughable. "Ladies, really, I think you've got the wrong girl. Trust me."

The redhead pulled her phone from her pocket and scrolled. "You're the one who's going to be on that show, right?"

"Yes, but..."

"Look"—the woman showed Rylee the face of her cell phone—"this video says it all."

With that, the woman pushed the button to start the video. It was a commercial about the show and the upcoming episode. Darius, looking fine in a black button-down shirt, spoke into the camera. He said he

185

was proud of this upcoming episode. He was particularly excited to help a young woman who was given the monumental task of following in her grandmother's footsteps. His opinion made her feel good. Somehow his approval meant so much. She couldn't help herself. She lifted her gaze to him, and he met her eyes with an appreciative look. *Zoom.*

"Here's the best part," one of the women said, and Rylee turned her attention back to the video.

It was a clip of her on the night at Jo-Jo's Java House. The first shot was of her outside picking up the big old hairball of a coat from the ground from where she'd thrown it. It showed her shrugging herself into it, the bag of her belongings from Freddie's apartment clutched in her hand. The ridiculous red purse that had been a birthday gift from her grandmother only served to make her look like a crazy bag lady.

Then the video went to the scene of her inside the coffee shop letting Darius pay for her coffee. The voice-over told of how *Wirth More* was proudest of helping someone who couldn't even pay for her own coffee.

What the hell! Rylee's insides squeezed, nearly choking all the air from her lungs.

Kit was at her side, wrapping her arm around Rylee's shoulders. She pulled her close and whispered, "Let's get out of here."

Darius came toward her from the bar. His face was contorted in concern, eyebrows pitched in on themselves, lush mouth pulled into a thin seam on his face. *Asshole.* All the venom that churned within her wanted her to go to him and unleash the wrath going on inside her. But she bit it back, drew blood in the effort.

Turning to the two women at her side, she manufactured a smile. They'd meant well, and with people from both the sponsor and the show still lingering nearby, she couldn't mouth off. This damn episode had to air. The damn contract said so. "Ladies, thank you for coming over to say hello. That video isn't exactly accurate, but the episode of the show should be fun to watch."

Then she turned to her friend. "Kit, ready?"

Kit grabbed their coats from the backs of their chairs, and they headed toward the door. Darius was there to greet them. "Not now, buddy," Kit said. She motioned her head to the onlooking crowd of people from their party. "If you know what's good for you. Not now."

His eyes implored Rylee. "Listen to me for just a minute."

She met his gaze and shot a hot whisper. "Go to hell."

Chapter Twenty-Seven

Back at her apartment Rylee and Kit sat on her sofa in silence. Rylee's mind reeled. How could he? How could he exploit her this way? What the hell was wrong with her that she actually thought Darius Wirth was one of the good ones?

"You want some wine or something?" Kit stood. "What do you have?"

"No, thanks. I just want this to be over. I can't believe we've got to film that damn fashion show. Why can't it be done already?"

The doorbell rang, and it jarred her insides. She caught Kit's gaze. "Can you get it? If it's him, tell him to go to hell."

"Gladly." Kit went to the door.

A moment later she returned, and the look on her face told Rylee she wasn't going to like what she had to say. Before any words could form on Rylee's lips, she saw there was someone standing behind Kit. Zen Angie. *Shoot me now.*

"Honey bun." Her mother dashed across the room to the couch and plopped herself down. "I saw the commercial. Dreadful. Just ridiculous. And whose coat was that you were wearing?"

"Mom." Rylee closed her eyes. She was suddenly bone tired. All she wanted was to be alone and hope that sleep would overtake her. "I can't talk about this now."

"Well, of course you don't want to. It's terrible is what it is."

"Um, I think maybe I should go," Kit said.

Rylee met her gaze and tried to convey that she wanted her to take Zen Angie with her. "I'm exhausted. I think maybe I'll just go to bed."

"You can go, Kit. I'm here now." Zen Angie tapped Rylee's knee.

All the years of her life when Rylee had needed her mother's undivided attention, all the moments when her grandmother had been the one to dry her tears or the one who had taken her shopping for a party dress, she had wished for her mother. But not now. Tonight even Rosie herself wouldn't have been able to make this go away.

"Mom, I appreciate you coming over. But I think I'm just going to take a shower and go to bed."

Rylee would not let that pout on her mother's face affect her. This was not about Angie and her fragile ego. As much as she'd craved a doting mother when she was a little girl, she didn't want that now. She wanted her dignity, and no, it was not in this apartment tonight.

Kit, back in her coat and scarf, leaned down and hugged Rylee. "I'll talk to you in the morning, friend. You sure you're good?"

She plastered on a big jack-o-lantern smile. "I'm ducky."

Kit turned to Angie. "Want to walk out with me?"
God bless you, Kit.
"I think I'll stick around a bit."
"Mom, it's okay. Really."

Rylee knew the drill. This was the part where the old Angie would have caused a scene, made it all about herself and rant about how her one and only ungrateful daughter had slighted her. But, no. Zen Angie settled herself on the sofa and folded her arms.

"Go take your shower, honey bun. I'll make us cups of tea."

After Kit left, Rylee went into the bathroom, tugged off her clothing as if she were mad at it, and stepped into a too-hot shower. She let the spray drench her, heat up her cold, cold skin, penetrating to the bone. Something about being in the shower made her think. It was a place where her mind opened up in the humidity.

The shower was like being in a tiled and wet confession booth. And the truth was that, yeah, that ad made her look pathetic, and in her life so far, she'd had plenty of pathetic moments. Now it was documented for all the world to see, so that was ducky. But she was angered and disappointed to her heart's capacity that Darius Wirth was a dickhead just like all the others.

She toweled off and wrapped herself in her chenille robe, pink with chocolate-brown hearts riddled all over it. A Christmas present from Rosie back a couple of years ago. She snuggled into it and willed her grandmother to impart some afterlife-to-earth wisdom, to fix this mess. All she heard, though, was Zen Angie's voice beyond the bathroom door. She was talking with someone, and she sounded smug and haughty, the keeper of the gate.

Rylee hadn't heard that bitter tone come from her mother in years now that meditation had become her daily practice. She stood by the closed door and listened. With each syllable that came through the door, her heart quickened. It was him. Darius. *Oh shit.*

She was tempted to climb out the bathroom window and slide down the drainpipe to her car and drive away forever, but then she remembered she wasn't in an episode of *The Three Stooges*. She had no choice but to face this guy. She cinched the belt of her robe and opened the bathroom door.

****

When he saw her, he looked relieved. Angie, however, hands on her hips, acting all mother hen-like, kind of made Rylee want to laugh. This was a fun new version of her mother. Maybe Angie would even slap Darius. One could hope.

"What are you doing here?" Rylee stood next to her mother. That felt good too. Partners in detest.

"I came to explain."

"I told him where he can shove his explanation." Angie stood tall, shoulders square.

"Mom, it's okay." She surprised herself with the calmness that had blanketed her. "I've got this. There are a couple of things I'd like to say to him."

"Oh, me too," Zen-Free Angie said. She fixed her stance.

Rylee put her hand on her mother's arm. "Mom, thank you. Really. But you go on home. I'll call you later."

Disappointment painted her face, but her mother was giving up. "If you're sure," she said quietly.

"Yes, Mom."

The whole time Rylee's eyes were on Darius. He looked like a deer caught in headlights, if deer were ever pirates.

Angie hugged Rylee and walked past Darius, but

not without first giving him a narrowed look. *Go, Angie.*

When she was gone, Rylee pressed her hands to her hips. "Look, I don't know why you bothered. If you're here to apologize, you can save it for someone who gives a crap."

"I did not do that voice-over."

"Yes, you did. I recognized your voice. I'm not an idiot."

"I did the early part of the footage, yes, the part where I talked about helping your store and helping you with taking over your grandmother's legacy. But that other stuff was all Jake. He's an ass, but, unfortunately, he's the boss and there's nothing I can do about him. I've already given him a piece of my mind about it. But there's no pulling it back. People are buzzing about the upcoming episode online and on the show's website. They can't wait for it to air."

"Well, bravo to you. Can you go now?"

"I'm sorry." Darius took a deep breath.

She could see his chest rise and then fall. Her heart tugged, and she admonished it for reacting to him. When he took a step closer, she put up her hand. "No. Darius, I mean it. It is what it is. Just go."

"Okay. I'll go. But not before I say this. Rylee, I've spent every day, every minute of every day since we've met trying to keep myself from thinking about you, wanting more, asking myself *what if*. What if there were no contract in place? What if we were free to do what we wanted? What happened between us was not a one-night lapse in judgment. I think you know that, even if you'd never admit it now. I like you. I really like you. And I hate this whole mess we've gotten ourselves into."

Rylee's insides began to unclench. She moved her hands to the knot of her robe's sash, as though hoping the tightness of it around her body would keep her from melting into a puddle.

Darius took a step closer, and she did not stop him.

"This is not what I signed up for when I came on board for the show," he said in a low voice, an intimate tell-you-a-secret sound. "I wanted to help people. Now that I really see what's going on around Sycamore River, I'm especially sure my original idea was a good one. I didn't count on the part of this TV show that would twist the truth just to get good ratings. And more importantly, I didn't count on meeting you."

"Please stop." The whisper escaped her lips. Her heart wanted to believe. It really did.

"I'm not the bad guy, Rylee."

She could not respond. There was a lump in her throat the size of a fist.

They shared a long look, and in that suspended moment all she wanted was her arms around him. She wanted to untie her robe and let it fall away. She wanted his fingertips on her skin, his lips on hers. But that was impossible.

"I, uh, want you to go." She filled her lungs with air and exhaled. "Just be gone, Darius. We'll film the fashion show and then just be gone. Can you do that? If you're not the damn bad guy, can you please just do that?"

His Adam's apple rose and fell in a swallow. His eyes were intense, dark, shiny, raw with something she couldn't read, yet it stole her breath.

Darius looked away. "Friday, then."

All she could manage was a nod, and in a breath he left. She was alone, just as she'd wanted to be all night. But now it was not solace that coursed through her blood. It was Darius Wirth.

Chapter Twenty-Eight

Days had gone by, and still Darius couldn't stand to give Jake more than a few syllables in response to his questions or comments. The more Jake pontificated in his usual spew, the more Darius saw him for what he was. A snake. Jake the snake.

The two of them sat in Jake's office going over the upcoming schedule for the final shoot at Rosie's Bridals, the fashion show.

"The reaction from that commercial is exploding all over social media. So you can stop pouting and thank me."

"I talked with Kit from Rosie's, and they are getting freaked about not receiving the delivery of the samples." Darius kept his eyes on his tablet. "Rylee got on the horn with the shipper, and of course they told her the order went out."

Jake chuckled without looking up from his tablet. "Putting our wacky shopkeeper in a tizzy, are we?"

"She needs time to catalogue the dresses and go over her runway commentary."

Jake looked up and grinned. "This is going to be great."

Darius could not speak around the fist in his throat. His mind pelted him with his own words. *I'm not the bad guy.*

Jake leaned in close. "This will be perfect. You'll

see. Turns out this screwb…uh, this Rylee person has kind of captured something in people. Pity, I'd guess. So don't sweat it. The samples will get there, and we, you specifically, are going to come out like the hero, as usual."

Jake's usage of the word *pity* gnawed at him. He shouldn't be feeling protective about Rylee, but he did. And he hated that viewers were playing right into Jake's intention for the disparaging commercial that continued to air.

The image of her that night in her apartment crowded his mind. The way she stared at him with discerning eyes. He could read what those green eyes of hers were saying, and unfortunately, he had to concur. He was an ass. But the connectedness to her was unrelenting. He felt it. She felt it. He knew. Maybe this latest disappointment should have severed it, but it didn't. Not for him, anyway.

"I'll be glad when this is a done deal and we lock in the second season," Jake said.

"Yeah, well, that's one thing we can agree on."

Chapter Twenty-Nine

By Wednesday the gown samples had still not arrived. Rylee got the same answer from the designer every time she called. They were shipped. Their paperwork said the dresses were delivered to her door. It made no sense. The designer said the shipment had been signed for but they couldn't read the signature.

She picked up her phone and dialed Darius's number.

"Rylee, hi."

"Look, I know you already told Kit yesterday that you're not worried about these gowns not being here for the shoot, but I'm borderline ballistic. I think we should cancel."

"We'll be fine, Rylee."

"How can you keep saying that? Darius, there are no gowns. You can't have a bridal fashion show with no bridal gowns. *Comprendo*? I say pull the plug."

"First off, there's no pulling the plug. It would be a breach of contract. I know you were concerned about writing up your commentary on the gowns, so take the info off your order sheet."

"That's all well and good, but it still doesn't produce dresses."

"Look, the guys are going to come to your shop first thing tomorrow morning to film the setup, film the models arriving and you and your staff talking with

197

them about the fashion show lineup and the delay in the dresses and such. I have an appointment at my father's nursing home first, and then I'll be at the store to go over things with you. On camera, of course."

"Of course," she spat. "My agreeing to be on your show was supposed to help Rosie's Bridals, and it's going to wind up burying us. Congratulations."

She pressed the Off button. One good thing about this whole mess was that soon she'd never have to see Darius Wirth again.

****

As soon as he walked through the front doorway of The Memory Center, Darius knew something was up. And as he made his way down the quiet corridor, medicinal smell crowding him, Toni from the finance department met him by the elevator. The look in her eyes told him there was news. He didn't hear any of the greeting that came from her mouth, and the response he uttered barely registered. What he did hear with crystal clarity was her next statement.

"Hilltop Manor in Chester has an available room for your father." Toni touched his arm. This was a nice, caring woman who knew Darius's trepidation about moving his father. "We have to act quickly, Darius. These rooms get snatched up fast."

The elevator arrived, and he let the cab sit there empty while he just stared at Toni. He knew this day was coming, and the place in Chester having a room for Pop was not a bad thing. He just felt as if he was letting the old guy down. This was Pop's home. These people knew him, really cared about him. Every single person in this place knew Pop's name. That said something.

"How long do I have before I have to give the go-ahead?"

Toni screwed her mouth sideways. "None." Then she brushed a hand up and down his arm. "I'm sorry, Darius. I know this is tough. But your father will do well at Hilltop, and the affordability will allow you to rest easy."

"Okay." What else could he say? There were no choices left. None.

****

Pop was up and in the reclining chair beside his bed. His hair was damp and combed back over his crown. Dressed in a navy-blue sweat suit, he looked clean and almost bright eyed in the morning light. Darius's heart lurched when his father met his gaze and cracked a jagged grin.

"Hey, Pop."

"Darius."

His heart whirred when the old man remembered his name right off the bat. He went over and sat himself on the newly made bed. "How are you today?"

"I ate."

"Yeah? What'd you have?"

"Scrambled eggs. The fake kind."

Darius laughed. Even in his state of mind, Mitch Wirth could tell the real thing from the imposter. "So, Pop, I have some news. We're going to move you to a new place. It's called Hilltop Manor in Chester, and I think you're going to like it."

"Move?"

"Yeah, it's not that far from here, actually."

"Why?"

Why, indeed. What could he say that would make his father understand? "It's time."

"Where's your mother?"

Darius blew out a long breath. With so much boomeranging around in his mind, he could explode.

"I'm going to talk with the people in the office and get the paperwork all straight, and then I'll come back and help you pack up. How's that?"

Martin Wirth stared him down with more perception in his gray-blue eyes than Darius had seen in a long time. Under that scrutiny, Darius felt like a mound of powdered-egg substitute.

"Pop, look. I know you like it here..."

Mitch nodded, but his gaze remained fixed.

"And I wish you could stay. I tried. Trust me."

"We"—Pop's head bobbled with an urgency to get his words out—"raised a trustworthy boy." He planted a garish grin on his trembling mouth. "You do right." His rheumy eyes misted over. "You do."

A tear stung the corner of his eye. He loved this old man.

Chapter Thirty

The entourage from *Wirth More* arrived right at nine in the morning. The guys with the cameras went to work setting up their lighting and such while Emma ushered in three tall skinny women Rylee assumed were the models for the nonexistent wedding gowns.

"Hello, Rylee. Here are our models. Tiffany, Lara, and Maeve." Emma waved a hand toward the towering women.

Were those hipbones poking through a cable-knit sweater on that one girl? How protrusive were they if Rylee could see them through the wooly shroud? *Wow.* She regretted that bagel she'd indulged in this morning. "Hi, ladies," she said. "Emma, any news on the samples?"

Emma shook her head. "Darius will be here soon. He'll have the scoop on them. Meanwhile, let's go over the mechanics of the show. Where are your helpers?"

Rylee didn't like the dismissive way Emma referred to Kit and Freda, as if they were elves holed up in a tree busily baking chocolate chip cookies. These women continued to save her ass day after day.

"Kit and the sales associates are back in the stockroom getting things ready."

"Okay, then, lead the way."

****

Darius took a tentative sip of his coffee. It was still

201

too hot. The crowd at Jo-Jo's had thinned now that it was well past the morning rush. He checked his watch. Almost eleven. Jake would be here any minute to discuss Friday's orchestration with the sample gowns. The plan would go off without a hitch. It always did. Just when Rylee would begin an apology to the fashion show attendees, he would swoop into Rosie's Bridals with the damn dresses. There'd be hoorays all around. Would Rylee see through it? See through him?

He was reminded of that look on his father's face earlier and the craggy words that had escaped from his throat. The only good thing about Alzheimer's was that Mitchell Wirth didn't have to know his son was not the trustworthy man he thought he was.

First thing Monday they'd move Pop to the new place. The place hadn't been all that bad when he'd visited it. Kind of old but kept up well enough. The problem, though, had been the staff, the residents, and the building's size. The facility was huge, impersonal, like a factory that produced old folks. Nobody looked the least bit happy either, but maybe he'd imagined it. Or maybe Pop wouldn't sense the discontent among the folks at Hilltop, but Darius would always see it. He saw the unhappiness now in his mind as he sipped his coffee. The obvious discontent gave him a burning sensation inside, as if he were drinking battery acid instead of the best java he knew.

The front door opened with a gust of chilliness, and Jake stepped into the coffee shop. He spread his arms wide when his gaze landed on Darius. "Show time!" He plopped himself onto a chair at Darius's table and tugged off his kid gloves. "Ready to do some hand-holding with the whack job?"

"What did I tell you about calling her that, Jake?" Darius's insides were on a slippery slope. Every word that came out of Jake's mouth just slammed home all the more what a cruddy thing they were doing for the sake of ratings.

"Hey, I'll stop just as long as you remember she's off limits to you, pal. I see the way you look at her. Personally, I don't see it. She does have a great ass— don't get me wrong—but I'm more of a blonde fan." Jake got up to order himself something with a "Need anything?"

Darius shook his head. He didn't even know where Jake had those samples stashed. And just thinking about how Emma had waited like a burglar outside Rosie's for the shipment made him ill. The coffee in his stomach sloshed around. This was all so ridiculous and for what? Admitting you were a fraud was no picnic. It was worse to know you were such with no good reason. Choices and consequences. Sometimes there was no good choice, yet one had to be made. Everywhere he turned, his hands were tied, as if choices were being made for him, forced down his throat like that mashed-up stuff his father had to endure at mealtimes.

He was sick of it. Sick of disappointing the people he cared about. For the first time he admitted that that included Rylee. He cared about her. Somehow he'd make this up to her, and he didn't give a shit about what that meant to the show.

His heart banged hard in his chest with new conviction. As far as Pop was concerned, there was a choice. There was one way to keep him at The Memory Center, and as much as he'd tried to avoid such an unpleasant choice, he was going to do whatever it took.

He picked up his phone and scrolled through a blur of names and numbers until he found what he was looking for. He hoped Armando Herrera was still an art collector in New York, and he hoped the guy still wanted the Mabel Alvarez painting.

****

Rylee and Kit sat in chairs at the worktable in the supply room while Judy, the makeup artist from *Wirth More*, applied powder and blush to their faces with adept strokes of her fat brushes.

"I'm going to miss this part," Kit said, and Judy smiled. "How nice would it be to have someone swoop in each day and doll me up?"

"If it means that much to you, I could slap on some gunk when you come to work in the morning," Rylee jibed. "It'll cost you a coffee, though."

"Ha," Kit said. "You avoiding Jo-Jo's these days?"

"Um, you mean since that wretched video blasted the internet? Yeah. Staying clear of the coffee place. And don't get me started on that, thank you very much."

"It's just show shit," Judy said in a conspiratorial whisper, leaning close with an eyebrow pencil. "Stay still a minute."

"*Show shit*. Nice. There's a lot of that going around."

"Oh, you mean the samples gowns?" Judy turned her pencil around to the brush side and scraped it along Rylee's brows. "Don't worry. It's just more bullcrap." She stepped back to examine her workmanship. "You have such a great natural arch."

Rylee pushed Judy's hand away when she came in with a shadow applicator. "What do you mean just more bullcrap?"

"Oh." Judy looked around and lowered her voice. "You did not hear it from me, okay? I can't afford to lose my job."

"That's fine. Just tell me what you meant."

"I heard from one of the assistants that the station manager—you know Emma, the one with the red-framed glasses—well, she apparently signed for the dresses when they arrived, and they've been holding them hostage someplace until the last minute to make a big splash for the fashion show. Boost ratings. When Darius gets here today, he'll come up with some plan B scenario and give you the *chin-up* pep talk. It's for drama. So when you shoot today's footage, act like you don't know it's just show shit. Oh, and you can cry. The mascara is waterproof."

"Are you serious?" Kit jumped off her stool. "They've been messing with us?"

"Oh God. Lower your voice, girl," Judy said. She indicated with the end of a brush. "And get back up there. I'm not done with you."

Rylee remembered Rosie's crazy apple-peeler machine that she used for making Thanksgiving pies. She could see Rosie with that look of consternation on her face as she cranked the handle while the apple, speared by a metal rod jabbed through its core, rotated around and around and the green skin peeled away in a coil. Her gut felt like that apple right now. All she'd ever thought about Darius Wirth peeled away and left her fleshy insides exposed, raw, and vulnerable to rot. What, oh what, would Rosie say about any of this right now? And, shit, what would she do?

"Let me get this straight, Judy," Rylee managed.

"Darius has had the samples all along, hiding them someplace?"

"Man, I've got a big mouth. I was trying to let you know it's all going to be okay, not make you mad. Stop biting your lip. You're screwing up the lipstick. Crap. I'm in trouble."

"Judy, I promise. No one's going to hear this from me," Rylee said. "But just tell me. That's what happened?"

"Yes." Judy blew out a breath. "He's going to bring them to the fashion show"—she drew brackets in the air with her fingers—"in the nick of time." She looked at her watch. "He'll be here any minute, though. So please, ladies, don't get me in trouble. Let me finish your makeup."

Rylee sat back on her stool and reached a hand over to Kit. She mouthed the word *crap* to which Kit mouthed *bastard.*

Rylee's insides continued to spiral around and around like an apple perched on its torture device. She thought of Rosie again. Her pride in this shop and the way she'd never let anyone know that the finances were subpar. And the old gal had somehow decided her granddaughter was the one to save the day. If Rylee weren't an apple on a spit right now, she'd laugh. An apple rotating around and around. *Ring Around a Rosy.* The image of the picture from the *Saturday Evening Post* affixed to Rosie's album of brides popped into her head.

Judy folded her arms. "You two are done. Don't touch your faces." She lowered her voice. "And don't forget." She put a finger to her lips. "Don't let on."

Rylee crossed a finger over her heart. "Your

secret's safe with us." While Judy packed up her gear, she poked Kit's arm. "I've got an idea."

Kit's lipsticked mouth curved into a full grin. "I like that look in your eyes, Ry. I see mischief."

"We have to work fast."

Chapter Thirty-One

Rylee was ready for him when he arrived. Judy touched up his finely chiseled, lying-ass face with some powder, sprayed his Superman hair, and the camera guys got into place. And Rylee forced a blank face while he recited his bullshit for the camera.

"Since the samples haven't arrived yet and the fashion show is just two days away, maybe we'd better discuss an alternative." Darius's obsidian eyes shone as if he were really concerned, and not just playing to the lens recording this mess.

"What do you suggest?" she asked. "Do we cancel?"

He blew out a long breath, put his hands on his hips, and looked around. "I'd hate to do that."

"Yeah. That would be a nightmare." She wanted to tell the truth to that camera, tell the audience what she knew, but she wouldn't. Aside from the fact that she'd taken that ten grand from the show and had put it to good use and had no way to pay it back if she broke the contract, Judy needed her job as the makeup artist. The guys with their cameras and all the other staff needed theirs as well. But Darius. She should blow the whistle on him. He deserved it.

She was disappointed on a gut level about this guy. This was worse than Freddie and his sudden declaration of love for the triangle banger. Darius Wirth killed the seed of belief that had started to grow in her, mowed it down like a tractor over a flowerbed. She was so done with men. Maybe she'd get some cats. And some M&M's.

"Well, let's keep our hopes up, but in case the samples don't arrive before the fashion show, let's do this." Darius reached into a box he'd placed on a chair. He withdrew a stack of what looked like pamphlets. He handed one to Rylee.

It was a flyer of models donning the designer dresses that were supposed to be here and brief descriptions of each one. Rylee scanned the pamphlet and then looked up at him. "So when these women arrive on Saturday, we hand them these papers and hope they won't be too disappointed that there's no fashion show after all?"

"We'll explain. You can introduce yourself, you know, greet everyone. We'll offer them refreshments, talk to them a bit about the new Rosie's and your vision. I'll go over it with you, help you write your speech."

She felt the camera on her, felt the beads of sweat forming at the back of her neck from the lights baking her. "Okay" was all she could manage. The pretense sat like yesterday's yogurt in her gut.

Darius patted her arm. "We'll make it work."

And that was a wrap. The crew began to pack up their stuff, and Rylee turned to walk away.

Darius touched her arm. "Rylee, wait a minute."

She faced him, her heart a ball of ice in her chest. She dared not utter a word, but many words, lots of them with just four letters, zipped around in her head.

"Let's take a minute to go over what you can say

209

on Saturday." He cast his gaze around the store while the workers were busy with their tasks. He lowered his voice. "And I'd like to talk with you about something."

She leaned in close and poked a finger to his chest where a heart should be. "Listen up, buddy. I wish I'd known how this was going to go down before I signed up for this mess. But since that's not an option now, let's just get through it, okay? I don't need you to help me write what I plan to say to these women who show up here for the fashion show. I've got this."

"Okay, that's fine. But can I talk to you for a minute? It's important."

"No," she said. "I'm done listening to anything you have to say."

****

Kit sat on the sofa in Rylee's living room and had that look on her face, a mug Rylee knew well. Her face said she was afraid Rylee was ready to bolt or switch gears, join the circus, take flying lessons. And she couldn't blame Kit. It was Rylee's modus operandi. The joke was that every time she had switched gears in the past, she always wound up back at the bridal shop seeking Rosie's comfort. Well, now here she was with nowhere to run.

Rylee brought a plate of cheese and crackers to the table. "I know what you're thinking," she said over her shoulder as she went back into the kitchen.

"I'm just waiting to hear your strategy."

She brought two glasses of white wine into the room, handed one to Kit, and sat beside her. She clinked her glass against Kit's. "Ready?"

"With baited breath."

"Okay." She took a sip of her wine and placed the

glass on the coffee table. "This is out there. I'll just say that up front."

"Why would I expect anything else from you, my friend?"

"But hear me out."

"All ears."

Rylee reached over for Rosie's thick binder of thank-yous from all the brides from over all the years. She ran her hand over the glossy vinyl cover that showed the picture from the *Saturday Evening Post*. *Ring Around a Rosy.*

"See this volume?"

"Yes," Kit said over the rim of her wineglass. "Rosie's memory book."

"All these brides." Rylee opened the front cover. She slowly turned pages as she spoke. "All this gratitude, all the stories, the love, the hope, the memories—this is what Rosie's is all about. And this is what we're going to give the women who show up on Saturday. History. Our calling card. Screw the new dresses and the pirate they're going to ride in on."

Kit put her glass down. "What are you going to do, though? I'm not sure I follow."

"We're going to get on our phones and hunt some of these former brides down. Lucky for us, Sycamore River has this way of keeping people close, so I'm sure we'll be able to locate enough of these women and let them know we need some help."

"We're going to ask them to what? Come in and tell the fashion show attendees that they were satisfied customers?"

Rylee nodded. "Yes! But we're going to ask them to be our models for the fashion show. Wear their dresses, tell their story, tell the new brides-to-be why they loved Rosie's bridals so much."

"Okay, but what if, you know, their dresses don't fit anymore. These women could be chunky now or pregnant. Then what?"

"Then they bring their dresses on hangers. See, Kit? It's more about their stories, their experiences here, than it is about the dresses. Get it?"

"And what do we do with the three stick figures the show provided for modeling the dresses?"

Rylee thought a moment and then snapped her fingers. "We throw some bridesmaids dresses on them and let them be attendants."

Kit just stared at her with wide eyes. For a millisecond Rylee's tendency to doubt herself trickled toward her heart. But she stopped it by scooting closer to Kit and leaning in close. "Please tell me what you're thinking."

Kit's eyes filled with tears, and she produced a grin. "Girl, you never cease to amaze. Let's get to work."

Then the doorbell rang.

****

Zen Angie breezed into the living room, wearing one of her handmade knit ponchos. As she peeled off her outer garments, she craned her neck to take in the scene. "Wine and cheese? Are we celebrating? Are we all ready for the fashion show on Saturday?"

"Getting there." Rylee flashed Kit a look she hoped read as a plea for silence. The last thing she needed was a prying Angie when time was so precious.

"Any more chardonnay?"

"Mom, we're kind of busy."

"I won't get in the way." She came into the room and took a seat in Rosie's wing chair. "I can help. Give me a job. I'm a good task girl." She turned to Kit. "Pour a bit of that wine, will you, Kit?"

"Look, I really appreciate your interest and all..." Rylee swallowed hard. She had spent so many days of her life trying to word her conversations with her mother in such a way that she didn't set her off. Sure, Angie was Zen now, but in the past few weeks, she'd seen hints of the witchy woman she'd been back in the day. She had no time to deal with this now.

Angie lifted her hands from where they were folded on her lap to the arms of the wing chair. She rested them there for a beat while she looked down at her empty lap, as though she were in prayer or meditating, maybe, hopefully. But then she looked up and pushed away from the chair. She pulled her poncho off the back of the chair and punched herself into it like a boxer's warm-up. She clutched her purse in her hand. "Okay, then." She marched to the door.

Rylee took in a deep breath. There would be time to sooth Mom's feathers later. She just couldn't do it now. She had work to do. "I'll call you later, Mom." She followed her mother to the door.

Angie nodded, her face contorted. It wasn't the wounded-victim look Rylee had been used to back over the years. This was not a Zen look either. This was anger, raw and real. She put her hand on the doorknob and opened the door. But she didn't walk through it. Instead, she shut it again and turned back to her daughter, eyes flashing with emotion. "I understand that you're busy, Rylee. And I know that right now the one person you'd love to have here to help you, guide you,

213

champion you is not me."

"Mom…"

"No. Let me finish. You want, you need my mother. Rosie was more of your mother than I ever was. I feel lousy about that now. I do. I really do. And thank God for Rosie for picking up the slack while I was busy with my head up my own ass." Angie clutched her purse to her body as if it were a baby. "But I'm here now, kid. Right here. I'm your mother. I want to be your mother."

Rylee's heart stalled in her chest, and she couldn't swallow save for the cinderblock in her throat.

"Let me," Angie whispered. Still Rylee could not speak. "I'm not good at the bridal business unless you count saying "I do" as many times as I have. And I can't show you how to make the best pie crust or anything Rosie used to do, but your mother is good for other things." She licked her lips. "Look, now you can make lentil soup."

Tears welled up in Rylee's eyes, and she swatted at the one that dribbled down her cheek.

"I see how much Rosie's bridals means to you," Angie continued. "I know I was skeptical when you first said that you wanted to keep the store. Maybe I was scared in a way. Scared that you really wouldn't ever need me." She shook her head. "Hey, I'm not Rosie, and I know that she'll always be the love of your life. But there's room for me too, isn't there?"

"Kit," Rylee croaked.

"Yes?"

"Pour my mom a glass of wine, would you? She's staying."

Angie smiled as she wiped the back of her hand

214

over her own wet cheek. "I'm so sorry about everything, honey bun."

"Thank you, Mom." She put her arm around her mother's shoulders. "Hey, you know a lot of people in town, right, Mom?"

"Me? Sure." Zen Angie clapped her hands and laced her fingers together as if she were about to pray. She cleared her throat and smiled. "I know everybody. Everybody! How can I help?"

"Come on." Rylee ushered her mother back into the room. "I'll show you."

Chapter Thirty-Two

Darius pulled the rental car into the parking lot of the show's building. It was a small vehicle, and the wrapped package took up the entire back seat. *Arabella in Repose* was sealed within the brown paper, ready to be delivered to Armando Herrera, who was scheduled to meet with him later today after the filming of the final episode at Rosie's Bridals.

It hurt to think that this legacy of his father's would wind up in a stranger's hands. Although a weighty decision, letting go of the portrait was the only way he could think of to keep his father in The Memory Center. Thankfully, his father wouldn't ever have to know the oil painting he loved so much was gone.

He locked the car and strode into the building, steeling himself in anticipation of Jake's smug mood. Determination thumped in his chest. Right now he could not believe he'd ever gone along with previous phony manipulations for the sake of the show's drama. But no more. As long as he lived, he'd never forget the look of disdain in Rylee's beautiful green eyes. Those eyes saw right through him, and they did not like what they took in, what they knew.

"Here he is," Jake said from behind his desk. "Our superhero. Did you remember your cape?"

He ignored the comment, and Jake's good mood only served to piss him off. "Everything all set?"

"No problem," Jake said with a sideways smile. "Easy as pie. The dresses are all in plastic bags in the back of the rental van. We'll head over to the store just as they begin to film the episode. How long do you think it will take your friend to make her apologies to the ladies who show up for the fashion show?"

"Not long."

"Five minutes, ten minutes? Come on, Darius. Timing's everything. You know that."

Darius blew out a breath and closed his eyes, regrouped his thoughts, tried to turn off the scoffing sounds in his head. "Ten minutes."

"What's wrong with you? Are you afraid this chick's going to wig out or screw it up somehow?"

"No, and shut up, would you?"

"You're acting like somebody stole your puppy. This isn't about the girl, is it? It's hands off for a long, long time, pal, so if that's the case, you should just get over it. She's cute, but so what? There's a whole world of good-looking, even better-looking, broads out there."

"Stop."

"Stop what?" Jake got up and came around the desk. He punched Darius's arm. "Come on. Let's go get the van and get this show on the road.

"I can't do this anymore, Jake."

"Okay, now you shut up." Jake shrugged into his jacket. He patted the pockets and pulled out a key on a ring. "Let's hit it."

"I mean it. This isn't what I want anymore."

"Really?" Jake stared at him with wide eyes. "Well, I have a contract that tells me otherwise."

"No, you don't. The contract is up after this episode, and if the sponsor wants another season, it's a whole new set of paperwork."

"What are you saying?"

Darius's heart thudded in his chest. Was he really saying this? The words tumbled from his lips. "I'm out."

"There's no time to debate this right now. We've got an episode to finish. Let's bring this nonsense up later over some beers. Okay?"

"We'll discuss it later, fine," Darius said. He followed Jake as they made their way to the van parked behind the building.

Jake swung open the double doors at the back of the van to check the dresses, which hung in zipper bags on a bar fastened to the insides of the cabin. Darius thought of Rylee back at the bridal shop getting ready to greet her customers-to-be and do some explaining. He hadn't seen the truth during the filming of previous episodes, but he saw it with full clarity today. This was bullshit. Unnecessary bullshit and he didn't want to be part of it anymore.

****

The small store was packed. No chair was left empty, and the narrow runway that came out from the workroom sat waiting. Rylee's heart did a dance in her chest. Her brain hummed. She was awed at how it had come together. She shared a look with Kit, and they gave each other a thumbs-up. Her mom sat on the window seat behind the chairs where brides-to-be waited for the show to begin. When their gazes locked, Mom winked. The truth was that Angie had been an amazing help while they hunted down former brides. Working side by side in this cause for Rosie's Bridals had done them both good. Rylee was sure Rosie herself was up there in Heaven enjoying the show.

"Ready?" Jimmy the cameraman said.

"As I'll ever be," she said.

Rylee looked down at her outfit, a pair of black trousers and a black turtleneck sweater. Her hair was pulled back in a tight high ponytail, sprayed slick by Judy's capable hands. She sported her silver hoop earrings and the charm bracelet Rosie had given her for her sixteenth birthday.

The three skinny models who were part of *Wirth More* agreed to wear the bridesmaids' dresses Rylee and Kit selected. Yeah, they were all "I don't know if the producer will approve, maybe we better ask him first" and all that, but Angie had been great at convincing them. She enjoyed standing by and watching Mom talk with the models and cajole them with her Zen-like verbiage. *Feel the flow of the fabric and compare it to the flow of this event. Free, easy, beautiful.* Go, Angie. The ribbon-adorned baskets filled with the pamphlets of the sample gowns slung over the models' narrow arms were a nice idea. Angie again.

Rylee held her note cards in her hands, and even though her knees were knocking, she felt good, sure. She tried her best to keep away the vision of Darius Wirth that knocked on the walls of her mind. But her brain would not cooperate. Periodically he'd appear in her head, dark eyes filled with emotion, his gorgeous mouth pulled down at the corners. She would not let him affect her. Not anymore.

The bridesmaids took their places in a line on the runway, and Rylee stepped up to the podium the show provided. From her periphery she could see the cameras on her and on the attendees. The heat of the lamps penetrated her skin. It was time.

"Welcome," she began, and a hush came over the crowded room. The silence unnerved her. All eyes were on her face, all eyes waited. She swallowed hard. "Thank you all for coming today to celebrate the reopening of Rosie's Bridals." She took a breath when she noticed her mother's eyes on her. Angie beamed.

"Unfortunately, due to some unforeseen glitch, the sample gowns have not yet arrived for our fashion show." She did her best not to stop dead at the murmuring among the women and the way heads turned to utter whispers. She'd get through this. This would work.

"Our models are wearing bridesmaid's gowns from the new collection of DeMonet Gowns, and you all can get a better look as they hand out pamphlets printed by the bridal designer. You'll see all the selections Rosie's Bridals will carry in the store, and we expect delivery soon." *Any minute by a lying snake.*

With that the models took their cue and paraded down the runway and gracefully stepped off at the end and began handing out the materials provided by the designer.

"Before you look at the gorgeous selections for the coming season, I'd like to say one thing. These wonderful dresses are not just available here at Rosie's Bridals. There are many, many bridal shops that can accommodate you if all you're looking for is the dress of your dreams. We have not cornered the market on dream dresses. But what we do have that sets us apart from the others is history. Let me take you on a little journey to the past."

Right on cue, the music softly began and the first

former bride stepped out from the back room and up onto the runway. Shelly Britton.

Shelly had lost weight since her wedding day and looked wonderful. The square-necked A-line gown was pinned close to her slimmer frame by Kit's expert hands. Shelly was radiant as she made her way down the runway and stopped at the end.

"Hi, everyone," she said in a tentative voice. She cleared her throat. "If you'd known me three years ago when I first came into Rosie's Bridals, you'd know how funny this is for me to be standing here today in front of all of you and not hiding behind a curtain. Let me tell you what this place means to me."

Shelly told her story of past insecurity and how Rosie had helped her feel more confident, helped her feel beautiful for her big day. Since then she'd used that newborn confidence to develop a healthier lifestyle, and she told the packed house how Rosie was instrumental in her new path.

Next was former bride Jenny McDade, who came out from the back room carrying her lace sheath on a satin-covered hanger. In her other arm, sitting at her hip, was a toddler, her daughter, who shyly sucked her thumb while her mommy paraded down the runway.

Jenny told the tale of how she'd been pregnant when she married her husband and with no close female relatives, had lacked guidance. Her inclination had been to purchase a gown that might camouflage a budding baby bump. But, no. After spending time at Rosie's Bridals and after many cups of herbal tea and rounds of chitchat, Jenny had decided on the revealing silhouette of the lace sheath. When everyone applauded her, the baby girl on her hip clapped her pudgy hands as well.

One by one, former brides walked down the runway and told their unique stories. When Megan Harris, the dark-haired beauty whose groom had been killed in a car wreck, made her way down the runway, the murmurs among the audience stopped. Many people in Sycamore River knew of her tragedy. Megan told her story of how Rosie had become a close friend and when she had found herself a widow, Rosie had been often at her side. She spoke of her gratitude to Rosie's Bridals for making her wedding day a memory that will always bring her comfort. The women seated in the rows of rented chairs passed travel-sized packages of tissues to each other, many dabbing at their eyes.

Kit came up behind Rylee and whispered into her ear. "There's a white van parked out back. Darius and Jake have been here for a while. They've been watching from the back room this whole time."

****

Darius listened to the last bride tell her tale. You could hear a pin drop in the room. The attendees were riveted to the stories these women had to tell. They'd even managed to have Jake keep his trap shut, which was monumental.

Finally, Jake spoke up. "Well, look at your flake saving the day, huh?" He poked Darius. "Now you go out there with this rack of samples and steal that thunder."

He'd had Jake's number from way back, but this behavior tipped the scales. Here was a man who knew nothing but opportunity, as long as it served him. Darius wanted to provide opportunity, but not for Jake or some paper manufacturer or for his own damn paycheck. He finally realized that, and it felt good.

Damn good.

"Come on," Jake prodded, as if Darius were a disobedient dog. "Get going."

"Oh, I plan to." He pushed through the doorway with the dresses swinging on the chrome pole of the wheeled cart.

"The samples," Emma called out in theatrical surprise from a corner of the room. "Rylee, the gowns have arrived!"

Darius wheeled the cart down the runway and stopped with enough room for him to walk around the cart and stand facing the seated guests. A round of applause sounded as he took a minibow before them. "Hello," he said with his winning-most smile. "Hello, everyone." His gaze found Rylee, and somehow she managed to keep from showing her disdain. But it was there. He felt it like a slap of her hand.

He talked about the dresses and the hard work of Rylee and her staff and then asked Rylee to join him on the platform. She came over with a smile on her face. She looked incredible in all black, ponytail swinging. She was sleek, feline, and his heart thumped with yearning and more. Pride. Rylee McDermott had pulled this off without the machinations of *Wirth More*.

After a few pleasantries Darius gave the floor to Rylee, who thanked everyone for coming, invited them to enjoy some refreshments and peruse the sample gowns. As she was doing so, a woman in the crowd stood up and raised her hand.

"Excuse me," she called from her place in the row. "Can I just say something?"

Rylee's face flushed hot as she looked over at the woman. "Gracie." The name rode from her lips on a whoosh of air.

The young woman squeezed past the ladies seated near her and came up onto the platform to stand beside Rylee. She leaned in and whispered to her. "Rylee, I hope this is okay."

The woman named Gracie faced the audience. "Hi." She uttered a nervous titter. "My name is Gracie Stern. I'm a Rosie's bride as well. My circumstance was that my dad was gravely ill, and in order to fulfill my lifelong dream of my daddy walking me down the aisle"—her voice hitched—"I needed a special favor. I needed to move my wedding up, and that required me to have a dress like in no time."

She looked over to Rylee and nudged her with her shoulder. "This lady here came up with the idea of my buying one of the samples. Apparently, this is a major problem for bridal shops, so don't even think about it. But in my case, in my need, it was Rylee who went to bat for me, made it happen. Granted, Rosie had to okay it, but it was Rylee who came to my rescue. I just wanted you all to know that Rosie's Bridals is in good hands with Rosie's granddaughter." She and Rylee embraced amidst a round of applause.

The brides-to-be and those with them moved to inspect the newly arrived dresses, then over to the display of cookies and flutes of sparkling cider. The mood in the room was upbeat, the energy high. This day was a success. And it had nothing at all to do with *Wirth More*. This day belonged to Rylee McDermott.

Soon the cameras had been turned off and the show's job was done. Darius found a moment to approach Rylee, who was replenishing the creamer at the coffee station. "You did a great job, Rylee."

She turned to him with cool eyes. "Uh-huh."

"We meet again amidst coffee and all its makings," he quipped. She did not bite.

"Is there something else?" She wiped her hands with a paper towel, wadded it, and tossed it into a trash can with a flourish. "Kind of busy."

"We, uh, we just got word the show is set to air next Friday."

"Okay." She shook her head. "Hope you get everything out of it you set out for."

Then she walked away. Darius watched Rylee engage with a new bride-to-be. She was a natural. Maybe she hadn't known it weeks ago when he first met her. But she knew it now. His heart lurched. Rylee hadn't needed the new gowns, and she sure as hell did not need him. Right now, though, he needed to meet the buyer of the painting and disappoint yet one more person on this godforsaken day.

Chapter Thirty-Three

The morning after the show aired, Darius was summoned to the offices of *Wirth More*. The episode was a hit, as he knew it would be, and everyone was celebrating. A continental breakfast spread was arrayed in the center of the conference table. The top brass of Parker Paper had been in negotiations with Jake and his minions, and they were on board for another season. Mimosas were handed out to everyone, and Jake made one of his self-aggrandizing speeches, thanking everyone but really giving credit to himself. The words went through Darius like a breeze escaping an open window. Just air.

When the group dissipated, Darius was left alone with Jake, and he was anxious to speak his mind.

Jake put an arm around Darius's shoulders and pulled him close. "We did it, man. We're in for another year."

"Jake, I meant what I said about being done. The show's going to have to be revamped, and I'm sure you'll find the right host. But me, I'm not signing on."

"You have to." The smile left Jake's face. He looked as if he might start swinging. "You owe me."

Darius let out a laugh. Everybody owed Jake in his mind. "I've paid up in full, Jake, and I'm walking away."

"And what are you going to do, huh? Without me,

what the hell do you think you're going to do that's going to give you enough dough to afford your lifestyle?" He folded his arms and angled his head.

"I'm going to do what I set out to do in the first place. Help businesses thrive."

"That's not going to keep you on the waterfront in Hoboken."

"You're right. And I'll tell you what, Jake. I'll give you right of first refusal. The unit's going up for sale, and if you'd like to buy it, it's yours. Market value. No more, no less."

"You're going to sell." It wasn't a question. "You're serious."

"I am."

"Why?"

"So I can be closer to my dad, who, thanks to the sale of my condo, will be able to stay in his facility."

"I thought you were selling that painting for the money."

"Can't sell the pinnacle of my family's heritage. It's history."

"Oh Christ, now you sound like the girl in the bridal shop. Life moves forward, buddy, not backward."

"That's where I'm headed, uh, buddy. Forward." Darius turned to leave and then looked back at Jake. "Let me know if you want the condo. First come, first served."

****

Rylee found herself alone in the store. Now that the show was behind her, she was officially open for business as the new proprietor of Rosie's Bridals. The episode had been good. Even she had to admit it. How

227

the editing people managed to make all that footage look like one sequential progression amazed her. Her shop was made to look good, and the part about the history was sentimental, and she was grateful that part of it didn't wind up being edited out.

She hadn't seen Darius in days. As much as she felt she'd grown, changed, over these last weeks, getting the wrong guy out of her head was going to take more time. She was just so sad that he'd turned out to be a louse.

The air outside was cold, and she was chilled to the bone despite the large mug of tea she had pressed between her hands. She'd pulled on Rosie's cardigan sweater, the scents of Rosie still wafting to meet her nose.

"We did it, Rosie," she whispered in the empty store. She put down the mug of tea and snuggled deeper in the sweater she wrapped around her frame. "Promise me you'll always be nearby helping me out."

The knock at the door startled her. Under the lamplight she saw the flash of Superman hair and the profile of his chiseled face. Darius.

She didn't have to let him in. This was her store. He knocked again and lifted his hand to show he was holding a cup of coffee from Jo-Jo's Java House.

If she turned away now, she would spend too much time wondering. Wondering what he had to say. She needed to put this to rest now. The only way to move past something was to look at it for real. She opened the door.

"Hi."

"Hi." Darius extended the coffee cup toward her. "Caramel macchiato."

"I have tea."

"Extra caramel."

The aroma teased her. She reached out and accepted the cup. "Thank you. But I'm sure you didn't come all this way just to bring me coffee."

"No, I did not."

They walked deeper into the store. She had only the desk lamp on, and the room was dim with pale light. Shadows did attractive things to the planes of Darius Wirth's face.

She took a pull of the pungent drink and put the cup down on the desk. "Darius, look, I'm grateful for what the show did for my store and all, but there's really nothing left to talk about."

"Let me say this, okay," he said. "Please."

It was hard to look away from those dark eyes. They sent a chill through her, and she wrapped Rosie's sweater tighter around her body. She waited.

"I did a lot of things wrong in the last couple of years. I'd forgotten who I am in here." He placed an open hand to his chest. "But meeting you, spending time, real time, with my father, and revisiting my hometown has done something to me. Made me remember."

Rylee swallowed hard. *Oh, please stop saying all the right things, Darius Wirth. I've only been a grownup for a few days, and I might forget to hate you.*

"I don't know what…"

"I quit the show."

"You what?"

"Quit. Oh, and I've sold my condo in Hoboken." He chuckled shyly. "Jake bought it. He's always wanted it anyway."

"Why would you do that?"

"Well, now I have the money to pay for my father to stay in The Memory Center. And I'll have enough to get a small place here in town."

"You're moving to Sycamore River?"

"Yes. I'm going to consult, find a way to help small independent businesses. Make a difference."

"Wow," she said, unable to process the news. "Wow."

"You knew about the delay in the dresses, didn't you?" he said. Before she could say anything, he held up a hand. "Don't tell me how you knew. I don't care. But when you talked about the history of this place and how important it has been, I just knew what I had to do." Darius took a step closer. "I almost sold my mother's portrait in order to get the money for my father's facility. But it was your talk at the fashion show that convinced me I was making a big mistake. So thank you."

Her throat was constricted, and she couldn't speak. And her heart thudded in her chest. She took a razorblade swallow. "That's a lot of news, Darius. Congratulations. I think?"

"Yes, congratulations are in order. I'm surer of what I want and where I'm headed than I've ever been. As a matter of fact, I'm headed up to The Memory Center now to bring my father the portrait. It's in the car I've been leasing. I figure it belongs to him. And for those moments when he comes back to us and knows who he is, I want him to see the portrait that started it all."

"That's…" She stopped for fear her voice would break. She swallowed. "That's great."

"I have two questions for you."

"Okay."

"Will you forgive me for being an ass and making a mess out of what you and I feel for each other? I've fallen in love with you, Rylee, and I think you love me too." He took a small step closer. "And if I promise to do better, will you take a chance on me?"

Rylee dug her hands into the sweater pockets, and the fingers of her left hand touched a piece of paper. She withdrew it. The post-it note from Rosie about Gracie Stern, the bride who wanted to buy a sample gown.

Well, Rosie, looks like you're still with me.

So Rylee said the words, the very words she knew by heart, the ones written on the little pale pink piece of paper bordered by rosebuds.

"Yes," she said. "Yes to it all!"

A word about the author...

Born to a feisty Italian mother and a gentle blue-eyed Irishman, award-winning author M. Kate Quinn draws on her quirky sense of humor, hopelessly romantic nature, highly developed sense of family and friendship, and her love for a good story while writing her novels.

Her Perennials Series began with *Summer Iris* (July 2010, The Wild Rose Press, Inc.), a Golden Quill Award finalist for Best First Book. The second, *Moonlight and Violet* (June 2011, The Wild Rose Press, Inc.) won the coveted Golden Leaf Award for Best Contemporary Novel 2011. The last in the series, *Brookside Daisy* (February 2012, The Wild Rose Press, Inc.) was a Golden Leaf Award finalist.

Her next project, The Ronan's Harbor Series, was a pair of romances set in a quaint shore town. The first installment, *Letters and Lace*, was released in June 2013 (The Wild Rose Press, Inc.). The second book in the series, *Restless Spirit*, was released in June 2015 (The Wild Rose Press, Inc.).

More information about these and other books by M. Kate Quinn can be found at www.mkatequinn.com.

M. Kate Quinn, a life-long native of New Jersey, makes her home in central Jersey with her husband. They enjoy big, raucous gatherings with their combined family of six (yes, six!) kids and their three perfect grandchildren.